Peter Benson was born in 1956. He is the author of four previous novels, most recently ODO'S HANGING. His first novel, THE LEVELS, won the Guardian Fiction Prize, his second, A LESSER DEPENDENCY, was co-winner of the Encore Award for 1989, and his third, THE OTHER OCCUPANT, won the Somerset Maugham Award. Both THE LEVELS and A LESSER DEPENDENCY have been adapted for BBC Television by the author, who has also had short stories published in anthologies and read on BBC Radio 4. Peter Benson lives in England.

SCEPTRE

Also by Peter Benson and available from Sceptre

Odo's Hanging

Riptide

PETER BENSON

Surfers Against Sewage (Campaigning for the benefit
of all recreational water users), The Old Counthouse,
Wheal Kitty, St Agnes, Cornwall TR5 0RE

First published in 1994 by Hodder and Stoughton
A division of Hodder Headline PLC

A Sceptre Paperback

10 9 8 7 6 5 4 3 2 1

Benson, Peter
Riptide
I Title
823.914 [F]
ISBN 0 340 62592 9

Printed and bound in Great Britain by
Cox and Wyman Ltd, Reading, Berkshire

Hodder and Stoughton
A Division of Hodder Headline PLC
338 Euston Road
London NW1 3BH

These things you keep
you better throw them away
turn your back
on your soulless days
once you were tethered
now you are free
once you were tethered
now you are free
that was the river
this is the sea.

Mike Scott

ONE

I got surfer's feet from my mother, and a fear of meat by-products. I got blue eyes and thin hair from her. I took a photograph of her and Dad on a Cornish beach from Marcus and Susan's photo album. Marcus and Susan, my uncle and aunt. I get a postcard from my mother every birthday, always from somewhere different, never more than two dozen words, never addressed. My room's at the back of the house, over the kitchen. There's surfing stuff on the walls: a wide shot of the Portuguese wave called Supertubes, stills from *Endless Summer*, Wingnut Weaver smiling on a Hawaiian beach, Tom Curren ripping Waimea Bay.

For my nineteenth birthday I was given a hundred quid, blank tapes, strawberry Sex Wax, a leash, my mother's postcard and I got the mistake she had to make. She had left the postcard for her hotel to post, and they had franked it RIVER COVE HOTEL, ST IVES, CORNWALL. I was shocked when I read this. Over breakfast I said, 'I think I'll go to Porthleven for a few days.'

'OK,' said Susan.

'Maybe a week.'

'Have you got enough money?'

Marcus already had his hand in his wallet. 'Here,' he said, and he passed me another fifty. 'Don't run out of petrol.'

'Thanks.'

'Don't thank me,' he said.

'Who should I thank?'

Marcus looked at Susan, Susan lowered her eyes and her face turned the colour of rain. She stood up and carried her cereal bowl to the sink. 'I'm not saying,' she said to the window, and her garden.

My Dad died when I was ten, in an accident at a pie factory. Someone somewhere ate part of my Dad, and that would have pleased him, because he was a generous man.

My mother couldn't cope with the nightmares that followed, shopping, other people's kitchens or me; she left me with her sister Susan and her husband Marcus, and their two children, and disappeared off the face of the earth. She has never been spoken about, it is as if she died and the postcard comes from beyond the grave. Smelling of damp, wormed earth, propelled through sulphurous air, over mountains and valleys I only know the names of, dropped on the doormat, lying face down. Maybe my mother is a ghost, maybe she always was. My nineteeth-birthday card was of a surfer slashing up on Fistral beach, and read, 'I always think of you when I'm in Cornwall. Happy Birthday, with all your mother's love.'

Once we were a happy family in Margate. We went on holiday twice a year, we lived in a big terraced house with a long garden, a view of the sea and more bedrooms than we needed, and we ate grapefruit and hot rolls for Sunday breakfast. We used to take evening walks along the promenade and sit outside a pub for a drink. Mother would howl with laughter at something Dad said, and he'd buy me two bags of crisps. He'd see people he knew and they'd wave as they passed, she'd admire his profile, and forgive his habit of looking at the waxy bits he found in his ears. He had big ears, and they were very hairy. Mother had ears like the little whorls you see on iced cakes, and thin lips that used to make me think of gardening. They were crinkled like the edge of rose petals, damp after a heavy dew. She had trouble with her hair; she never knew what to do with it. One week it was up and brown, the next it was down and coloured a lighter shade. Then she had it cut off and wore it like a man; tired of that she didn't go near a hairdresser for six months, letting it grow long again. Then, at the first opportunity, she had it permed. I think different hair kept Dad excited, not knowing what sort of head he was going to wake up to next. Maybe remembering one and then finding another; who knows now?

Apart from the hair and its changes, my memories of my mother are broken in pieces, so when I recall them, I see only edges of the complete picture. Here are her whorly ears, and here's the edge of her voice, telling me to eat cabbage. And here is the edge of her dress, curling over me. The edge of her touch, my head folding into her, or her hands on my back. The scent of Peau d'Espagne on her neck blowing towards me on a steady onshore wind. A knowing look on her long, thin face. Some surfers search for the perfect ride on an empty wave that runs for ever, barrelling over a smooth and kind reef, but I search for my mother. Here is her hand, raised and waving from a beach, and here her back at a kitchen sink, and me ready for school. There's a curl of black hair, or is it russet, or blonde? I'm pulling it out of a plate of macaroni cheese and dropping it quietly on the floor.

My memories of my Dad are fixed, frozen in places; on a beach in Cornwall, in a guest house that smelt of lard, steadying a ladder he was climbing, passing him an oil can when he was trying to fix a squeaky kitchen stool, walking the cliffs, at home watching telly, him coming home from work with flowers and a book for Mother. Him pushing me out on my first board – a log – one he made from a door.

There's not much surf at Margate, but down the road, at Joss Bay, the waves are the best in Kent. I saw my first big wave there. It was short but it tubed perfectly, and as I watched it someone I hadn't noticed suddenly appeared. A surfer.

He was awesome, dressed in a plain black wet-suit, riding an orange and white thruster. He lived inside each wave he caught, low and perfectly balanced for each radical manoeuvre. He spoke to the water and it talked back to him. The sun was hot and the sea was blue. Seagulls drifted above him, inclining their heads, riding the thermals, adjusting their positions with small movements of their tails. The surfer pumped down on his board and turned around on his waves. As he approached the shore he died as the surf died, disappearing beneath it and coming up smiling. His smile was small and peeped out from his mouth like carefully considered words. 'I want to do that,' I said. That was the only excuse Dad needed.

Dad let the car stand out all winter while he made the board in the garage. First, he beat the door to death with a claw-hammer, then unscrewed the hinges, the lock and the handles, and sawed the panel to a rough shape. He took a plane and began to shave the edges; he was a perfectionist, and spent weeks getting the shape just right. And when it was exactly right, he bought a can of varnish the size of a grown man's head and gave the board four coats. He sanded between each coat; my Dad's board was heavy, and its balance was screwed from the moment it stopped being a door, but I used it for three seasons and it never maxed me out.

The holidays were always spent by the sea. Weymouth, Dawlish, Newquay, Porthleven, St Ives, Salcombe, Sennen Cove, Bude, Exmouth; we stayed in all these places, usually in bed-and-breakfast houses run by middle-aged women and their pets.

I was seven when the board was made, and we tried it first

at Bude. I paddled out over sluggish breaks until I was caught by a mellow that turned me round and the nose of the board up. The board said 'Go', and I said 'Now'. I was instinctive, I wore thick blue trunks, I stood up, grew my first erection and, for five or six seconds, I rode my first wave. I was hooked. I looked towards the beach. My Dad was jumping up and down. My mother waved. She was holding a fat novel in her free hand. I put up my hand. The sun was hot. The board sank.

I still feel those five or six seconds. As the sea rushed beneath me, I was singing through my feet, and the board amplified my song through the water. The song was from *Porgy and Bess*, the words were in the sea and the melody was whistled by my Dad, given trills Gershwin had never intended. I don't know: 'Summertime', 'A woman is a sometime thing', 'One of dese mornings you goin' to rise up singin''? One of these or another? I saw the whole sky shine, and other surfers, riding behind and above me, appeared like members of the chorus. A single gull soared over me, and each cloud hung as if attached by cotton. The sea crested over the nose of the board, and when I shifted my weight forward, I accelerated. I leaned back and slowed, I heard the wake I left; when I focused on the beach, the people there looked as though they were illuminated by spotlights. I felt lit within, I felt immortal; at that time, my mother never had a passion as I had surf. This was her tragedy, and the reason she could not cope. Surf was my salvation. I lost my Dad but found him again in the ocean, and his song was mine, and that song sang from my feet.

In bed. You haven't seen your mother for eight years. She left you without explanation. You might meet her the following day. What are you going to ask her? What are you going to tell her? What is she going to say to you? Is she waiting for you? I have been waiting for this moment, and have no answers.

When I was left with Marcus and Susan, I pushed the shock and misery deep with one thing that could not be taken from me. They live at Norman's Bay, Sussex, where there is always a good swell, but not always good waves. It's always enough though, and I became king of the deliberate wipeout, and this took my grief away.

You wipeout when you fall off your board; I could take a wave and hold it in my hand, I would be able to teach it Greek, introduce it to my Geography teacher, call it names or take it on holiday; I would be able to ride it to shore but instead I'd lean forward, grab the nose and flip the board over my head, falling backwards over the lip and down the back of the wave, out of sight, with nothing but a strip of sky above me and folds of sea on either side. These elements were my clothes, I do not feel the cold. Physical cold is grief's brother, and my brother is my board. I am not sentimental about my board, my eyes, my balance, my low centre of gravity, my big, wide feet, waves or the combined power of these things.

What is this power? It is the power of forgetting, wipeout of the mind. Great surfers have died in wipeout, beaten by the waves, sunk by it and crushed by tons of falling water. The air is stolen from their lungs, they have lost consciousness and slammed into the sea bed and filled with sand. Sometimes their bodies are not found. Fit men with brown bodies and women ashore. The sea is a killer, and feathers and lead. You are in a doctor's waiting room and a woman comes in. She has a bone to pick with the doctor and shouts at the receptionist for five minutes before sitting down next to you. She's about twenty-one. She has long, straight blonde hair, and is wearing tiny pearl ear-rings. Her nails are painted pink and beautifully manicured. Her eyes are blue and do not blink. She is carrying a small dog beneath a smart black coat. The dog is beautifully groomed. The waiting room is hot, you feel faint, you have to blow your nose but you haven't got a tissue. You look at the woman's knees, then her hands, her arms, her neck, then her face. She is waiting for you to look in her eyes, and when you do she smiles. The smile is an old woman's smile, her teeth are brown, and she has a diseased tongue. This is the sea.

Can't sleep. 'I always think of you when I'm in Cornwall.' I wonder if she knew the hotel would frank the card. She could not bring herself to tell me where she was, as she could not bring herself to bring me up alone. The River Cove Hotel had to tell me, people I have never met. She makes me angry, and I can't get the anger out of my head. It picks at my mind and strips it of reason; I turned on the light, sat up and studied her handwriting. Was there something in the slope of her letters that gave me another clue, or the way she dots her i's? The dots appear over the letter in front, like spume flying off the crest of a wave, though the waves pull against the current. Is she sad or is she threatened?

I couldn't sleep, so I dressed and crept out of the house. Marcus was snoring lightly in his bedroom, Susan was still up. As I passed her room, she came to the door and said, 'Can't sleep?' It was as if she had been waiting for me.

'No.'

'Going to the beach?'

'Yeah,' I said.

'Want some company?' She reached out and touched my hand. She was cold.

'Dunno.'

'Come on,' she said.

'OK.'

Susan and I walked together in the moonlight. It was a still night, warm, and it smelt of sugar. Sugar in molten columns that rose from the earth and pierced the sky. Susan took my arm, and we walked slowly from the house to the beach.

Susan has never told a lie. She and Marcus are honest, they never fooled themselves into loving me as their own. Their children – my cousins – are older and different to me. Ronald is a doctor in Australia, Isabel is in Manchester and works in retail sales. Marcus is in insurance, and his hobby is insurance. Susan's passion is her garden, more sand and pebbles than flowers, but she grows huge potatoes and onions the size of footballs.

'Duncan?' she said.

'Yeah?'

'I saw the card.'

'Did you?'

'When you go down, are you going to try and see her?'

'Yeah.' I coughed and wiped my mouth with the back of my hand. 'If she's there.'

'If you do,' she said, and she turned towards me so the moon haloed behind her head, 'give her my love.'

'Of course. Anything else?'

She looked into my eyes, and there was no doubting them. 'I never told you before, maybe it's time to,' she said. She swallowed. Her eyes looked cast in steel, and glittered at their corners. The sea dragged the beach to itself, and threw what it didn't want back. It sounded as if it was unwrapping parcels of china and bells in front of a crackling fire.

'Told me what?' I said.

'I was sworn,' she stuttered, 'to secrecy.'

'Told me what?'

She held my eyes and did not flinch. 'I've never broken an oath,' she said.

'Are you going to now?'

'I think . . .' she faltered.

'You think?'

'It's a big thing for me . . .

'What?'

'. . . but I think it's more important that I break this one than keep it.'

'What is it, Susan?'

'Diana.'

Diana is my mother. 'What about her?'

'For the last eight years, she's sent me money for you. That fifty this morning; that was from her. And the money for your car. Most of that came from her.'

'You've known where she was?'

'Not all the time. She's moved a lot.' She coughed to clear her throat. 'She's never told me exactly what she's been doing, but I can read between the lines.'

'And?' I'm not angry, but I'm amazed. I understand that Susan took an oath, and how she must feel now. I feel that I'm about to catch a wave the size of a street.

'And she's found a man.'

'A man?' The wave lifted me up and I rose with it, climbing the water as if it was rock and I was wearing suckers on my feet.

'A man.'

'Who?'

'I don't know his name,' she said. 'I don't know anything about him.'

'No?' The wave was solid but moved as if it was water, flecked with spit and blood.

'No.'

'Oh,' I whispered.

'I'm sorry.'

'Why?' The wave began to curl above me and barrel behind; the faster I moved the faster it moved, and I heard it whispering about dealing with me. I kicked up and back, flew into the air and dropped down behind it. 'You don't have to be,' I said.

'No,' she said.

How do I feel? I expected this day, so I did not force it. I am patient. Surf teaches patience, anticipation and faith. It displays calm in fury. Below us, as we walked, the sea swept on to the beach in long, shallow sets. Fairy's surf. When the moonlight hit the lip of each wave it flashed along its length, unravelling into the night. Gobs of spume flew up and disappeared into the dark. I tasted salt in my mouth and my ears began to ring. Night surfing, I break the rules. The ringing stopped. 'Come on,' she said, and she took my arm again, and we walked across the pebbles to the tide-line.

A fisherman was sitting on a stool, six feet from the water's edge, his unshaven face lit by a hissing gas lamp. As we passed, he didn't take his eyes from the top of his rod. His line was taut, and dissolved into the dark, then the sea, weighted and baited at the end. The fisherman held a dead cigarette between his teeth. A miasma of guts and luncheon meat hung around him. He had erected a canvas wind-break, and wore a heavy waterproof cape. His rod was supported by a cradle, but he kept his hands on it. His fingers clasped and unclasped, otherwise he was motionless. He had a box of food on the beach beside him and a flask. The wind-break cracked in the breeze, and his line whistled softly.

'She told you about him in a letter?' I said.

'Yes.'

'Where from?'

'Essex,' she said. 'I think he was working there.'

'You said you didn't know anything about him . . .'

'I don't, Duncan. I was just reading between the lines.'

'Do you remember how the lines went?'

'No. Not precisely.'

'Imprecisely?'

'No, Duncan. I've already told you too much . . .'

'That means you haven't told me everything.'

Susan stopped walking. 'She told me,' she took a deep

breath, 'that she loved him. That's it.'

Essex. There're waves there, but they're broken things, fragile, dead-blown, that lapse towards the shore, insecure and paranoid. Those shores are lost to me. They are starved, thin as cats, grey and cold; if you offered them love they would spit it back in your face. I would not take my board to Essex, but I would follow my mother there. If she is being hassled I will be there.

She was staying in Southend. Remember? We went there.'

I remember. How could I forget Southend v. York at Roots Hall, where the birds fly upside down because there's nowt worth shitting on. The sight of a Southend striker bearing down on goal, three boys and an old man standing by the hot-dog stall at the back of the empty terrace, the cheers of thirty dedicated supporters rattling the loose rivets that held up the roof. Marcus took me to the match. We were walking past the ground when the gates opened, and the gateman pleaded with us to buy tickets. Marcus takes pity easily; he said, 'OK,' and offered the bloke a twenty-quid note for two on the home terrace. 'No,' said the gateman, looking at the note, 'I only wanted you to buy a couple of tickets, not the whole club.'

Half-way through the match it began to rain, and it rained in solid sheets and pooled on the pitch. The ball skidded and stopped as it was passed, so men who had not expected to find it at their feet found it at their feet and were forced to do something about it. Ball games give the player too much time to think, the best decisions are made without the luxury of time. Team games give the player too many chances to make excuses. Those Southend footballers did not like the conditions, they ran from them and lost 5–0.

'What was she doing there?' I said.

'She didn't say.'

'What's she been doing since she left me?'

'I don't know. She had some compensation, and she sold

the house, so she had some money. She travelled a lot. I had cards from lots of different places. Spain, Ireland, Canada, New Zealand. I think she was trying to lose herself, or find herself. I never knew which.'

I never knew which. Susan's straight, she doesn't worry herself. Other people mostly baffle her. She doesn't smoke and she rarely drinks, she eats plain food and never wears patterned clothes. Her bafflement has bred the ability to cut to the heart of some things; I was in a pub with her, and two blokes were steaming. They had insulted the barmaid, they had broken glasses, and were fooling around on the tables. No one was going to sort them out, so Susan stood up and forced herself between them and demanded to know why they were ruining everyone else's evening. For a moment, they were transfixed, amazed that anyone should ask them the question. And a middle-aged woman in plain brown clothes with a handbag in her hand. She wore no jewellery, she wore flat shoes, and no make-up. One of the blokes turned to his mate and said, 'What's the boiler on about?' Susan did not flinch. She said, 'I beg your pardon?' God, the two blokes laughed, then they dropped their laughs like stones and looked serious. Mean. Time in the pub was caught like a breath, or like the moment before a fast wave breaks and you have no time to stretch from prone to standing; the sea is roaring but you hear nothing. 'I beg your pardon?' one bloke mouthed. 'I beg your pardon?' said the other. They banged their heads together and then turned to stare at Susan. She stared back, put her hand to her shoulder and flicked away a ball of fluff. 'You're annoying people,' she said, and now she leant towards them and said, 'Nobody wants you here, so I think you'd better leave.' All the people in the pub stiffened, the stiffening could be felt in the air, the barman stepped from behind the bar with a baseball bat. Susan looked at him, then at her feet, then tapped her handbag with the palm of her hand and came back to where I was sitting. Susan drinks tonic water with a slice of lemon and sucks the slice dry when she's finished. The blokes left, promising to be back, but they never were.

I have never thought of her as my mother, just the woman I stayed with until I found my mother. 'I'm sorry,' she said. 'I broke my promise to Diana, and I'm afraid for you.'

'Why?'

'I can't say. It's between you and her; I've got nothing to do with it.'

'Only that you looked after me ten years.'

'Your mother suffered ten years, more than I know. She always did, even when she was a baby . . .'

'Everyone suffers.'

'Everyone can hear,' said Susan, 'but some can't enjoy music. They actually don't understand it. Can you believe that?'

'What's that got to do with Mother?'

'I've never heard you call her Mum.'

'I can't,' I said.

'That's it?'

'Yes.'

'Yes . . .'

'Did you ever think about telling me all this before?'

'Yes.'

'Why didn't you?'

'I promised her . . .'

'You've broken it now.'

'I had to one day; the time had to be right for you. I think she knows it too, and knew the hotel would stamp the card. She couldn't tell you herself, and at this moment she's sitting in her room, knowing we're having this conversation, knowing she's going to have to face you.'

'You think so?'

'It's possible. Anything's possible with Diana. She's never done the expected.'

'Maybe the expected never happened to her. Dad going like that . . .'

'The expected rarely happens to anyone,' said Susan.

'And I want her.'

TWO

I want my mother, but I also want to find a particular woman. She's got flesh, and this shows in wavy folds of skin, especially concentrated around her waist and stomach. A woman with a low centre of gravity, small feet, brown eyes and large breasts. I don't mind underarm hair and I don't mind big hands, but they must be soft. Pale, moist lips would be nice, and a big voice. I don't want shouting but I want lots of grunting and moaning. I'll grunt and I'll moan, and I'll sing through my feet.

I want to surf a woman. I want to be able to lose sight of my feet in her flesh, I want to try forward bottom turns, backhands off the lips, backhand re-entries and long, dangerous tube rides. I want bounce and I want slapping. I don't want it at any cost, or in the dark. I want to disappear as I do it and come out the other side with my arms up, perfectly balanced. I want rushing in my ears, damp hair and big, fat, hard nipples. I do not want to be blinded by sex, I want to be wiped out. Flattened by it for a moment, then I could flip back, stand again and catch another wave. I want sweat in her creases, I want damp hair, I want thighs like a meal and I know what I don't want. I don't want some redheads, some blondes, some Australians, most women who show any interest in team sports, or some African witch-doctor's daughters. Girls with cruel eyes who work in chemist's shops, girls with bitten fingernails who work in petrol stations. Nurses with no breasts and goat's eyes at drunk parties; chain-smoking students with short hair and a ticket to fourteen inland European cities. Girls on juice with yellow hair and quiet voices. Pass the tissues.

Norman's Bay at six in the morning. The sun rose from the sea and lit a heavy, broken swell. The sea was grey and cold, the waves were choppy, gulls dipped over a pair of fishing boats, the wind was a stiff onshore, the Beetle started first time.

When you sit in a Beetle, you wear it. Volkswagen built them to fit, and you can hear them coming for miles. This suited me. I wanted to give my mother plenty of warning, but I didn't phone, and I made Susan promise not to phone, or tell Marcus what I was doing. I thought: she's broken one promise, maybe she enjoyed the feeling and wants to do it again. Within weeks she'll be shoplifting, then she'll be having an affair, then she'll murder. Or not. Maybe. Who knows.

Marcus was asleep when I left the house, but Susan was up, and made me promise to ring when I got to River Cove. She worries. Promises, promises, so many promises. Possibilities, possibilities, there are too many possibilities, and they all converge at death wearing their best clothes, smiling.

'Don't forget,' said Susan.

'I won't.'

'And don't tell her that I broke my promise . . .'

'Don't worry,' I said. I kissed Susan on the cheek. She never wears scent. She patted my shoulder and stood at the gate to watch me drive away, her hand in the air until I was out of sight, and probably long after I had disappeared around the corner and down the road that runs alongside the railway line.

A Beetle's roof could have been designed to carry surfboards, and as I drove mine hummed to itself as it cut through the air. It's a six-foot, six-inch, three-finned Hot Tuna thruster, off the peg, medium weight. It's not the board that does the surfing, it's the surfer; a blend of balance and feet, waves and swell. I don't believe that a custom-made board gives the man the edge; a bad man has no edge, he just lacks skill. Skill is learnt but talent is bred; Hot Tuna of Australia make the boards for me, as if they knew who I was. I buy them off the rack; the last one I got at the Low Pressure shop in Notting Hill. I'm not sentimental about it, I haven't given it a name. It's a lump of cloth and resin-covered foam, pointed at both ends, with a big yellow and pink gaping fish decal at the nose.

I had breakfast at Bosham, Sussex, at a café on the front, with the sea washing the road beneath me, and an old woman opposite getting her milk bottles off the step before they disappeared. Bosham is flooded by high tides; there is no surf there, but it's a pretty place, with an ancient church and narrow streets of old houses. Here, King Canute tried to turn back the tide, persuaded by his men that he had the power, but he hadn't. His throne was carried to the beach, he was sat down, he was made a fool. I ate toast and marmalade, drank orange juice and two cups of coffee. There is no truth in the rumour that coffee destroys the vitamin C content of orange juice.

No surf at Bosham, but it's a beautiful, calm place, especially early in the morning. Wading birds patrol the mud-flats, dinghies bob at their moorings, retired men in big shorts row out in tenders to their cruisers. A pair of canoeists paddled down the estuary and turned into a hidden inlet. I asked for more coffee, and the waitress filled my cup without charge. She was my age and though she had some rolls around her waist, it wasn't enough. It was nothing; the slim waves that run along the shore on a still day. Nothing at all.

Dad, my mother and I never holidayed at Bosham, but we did visit Weymouth. I stopped at Weymouth for more coffee as I drove to meet my mother. I found a café we had visited, but I didn't recognise anyone from that time. The place had been redecorated, but the tables and chairs were the same. I sat by a window and watched fishermen mending their nets. The beach is clean, there are quayside attractions, a Punch and Judy, big hotels, lines of deckchairs along the front, and a statue of King George III, erected by grateful citizens of the town. People were reading books, eating ice-creams, or watching board-sailors.

There is some surf at Weymouth, but it's weak; the bay is a board-sailor's domain. I watched them for a while, and thought about the size of a fish's brain and the stuff in mine.

When we were on holiday, and Dad encouraged my surfing from the beach, Mother sat on the beach and read a book, or tanned herself, or paddled in the shallows. She was thin and she was elegant, with high cheek-bones and slim, pencilly fingers. She always wore a black one-piece swimming costume. I never saw her in anything different. She looked cool, quiet and in control. That holiday, I remember, she wore her hair short, it was black and curled down into sideburns, like a man's. She wore a big straw hat. She disliked newspapers but read classic novels. She annoyed Dad by always doing more crossword clues than he did, and she cooked great omelettes.

Dawlish Warren in Devon, across the Exe estuary from Exmouth, has good surf when you can catch it, but mostly it's broken stuff, difficult to catch and fast if you do. There are dangerous and manic rip-currents that burn out from the estuary, and constantly shifting sandbanks that confuse locals. It's an expert's sea; I spent my first holiday with a proper board at Dawlish; after three seasons with Dad's home-made log, I amazed myself. This new board was a Six-Six Hot Tuna, no slouch, half the weight of the log. After basic bottom turns and cutbacks, I taught myself to surf off the lip of fast-breaking rollers, fat waves with dangerous hearts and dead souls. If every beach is a street and every wave a house, every foot of wave is a person. A wave changes every foot, or maybe it doesn't, depending on the mood, the day or the place. Dawlish is a place where thieves hang out in the water. They will steal your Waterboys tour jacket, but not wear it with pride, they will be happy to pick its seams and then watch as it shreds off their back. Happiness for a Dawlish wave is a dead surfer, belly up, floating the wrong way with a broken leash still attached to his ankle. Bloated belly, crabs at his eyes, purple extremities.

There is a small amusement park behind the Dawlish dunes; I parked up and wandered down to the shore. I bought a cup of tea and a cheese roll, and sat on the front to eat and watch the rollers break along the beach. There were some surfers out, but they weren't picking up anything. They dropped in and out like flies; buzzing, persistent and patient. For thirty seconds, one caught a break that carried him long enough for a simple cutback, but then he fell, his board flipped over his head and shot towards the beach. I saw his head go under and then his feet go up; it was a sad day.

Dad, my mother and I stayed in a small hotel; I remember the same old scene. Dad and I on the beach, mother sitting on a café terrace, reading a long novel about Russia, looking up every now and again to wave to me, but never losing her place in the story.

I can recall her face, the shape of her body, her lips on my cheek and the smell of her scent, but I cannot recall her exact voice. It was clipped and proper, but there was something else to it. Disillusion? Pain? Loss? As I ate my roll, I listened to voices around me; one high-pitched whine here, a growl there, irritation in another. A mother strolled by, hand in hand with her small son. The child was whimpering, the woman said, 'Don't worry. We'll get it cleaned up.' The voice was soothing but tinged with panic, the son was bleeding from a cut knee. Had my mother ever spoken to me like that? I couldn't remember. Had I ever cut my knee? I don't remember. I think that if I had, Dad would have done the soothing and calming. I remember his voice perfectly; it was always level and always deep. I never heard it raised, he never lost his temper with me. And mother was patient and on holiday, and the memories piled one upon another like a building on the sea, and all the streets around it were empty.

I didn't stop again before River Cove, though I drove past other places we had holidayed. Torquay, Looe, then across Cornwall to Newquay. I wanted to stop and check the surf at Fistral, but it was getting late, and I couldn't wait. The closer I got to my mother, the larger she grew in my head, so the jumbled pieces of her pulled themselves together as images blend in a dream. Here's her hair, lighter and shorter than ever; here are lines on her face, lines she never had before. Here is the surprise on her face as she sees me coming, and the first answer to my first question. Here she is, introducing me to her man, hoping I'll like him. Here are my hands, sweaty on the Beetle's steering-wheel, and a scene from a Marx brother's film. An elegant woman pulls up outside a hotel in a Beetle, and asks Harpo to bring her luggage up to her room. Harpo opens the boot and shrugs. Cut to Harpo staggering down the hotel corridor, carrying the Beetle's engine. He enters the bedroom and puts the engine on the woman's bed. There's oil and grease everywhere, it's a laugh. The River Cove Hotel was around the bend. It was set high on the cliff, and raging, unsurfable sea pounded the rocks below every bedroom window.

THREE

I parked. It was seven in the evening. Light clouds were drifting from the west, and the sun was slowly sinking, the sky in its wake beginning to turn pink. The noise of the sea on the rocks came and went, like noise comes and goes in the drifty time before sleep. A door opens, a door closes, someone creeps upon a stair. Cats whine outside and a dog barks. Wind rattles a window-pane, the moon shines a damp road and cuts slices in a dark place. The cliffs crumble quietly, dropping their pieces hundreds of feet. The stair doesn't creak, the footsteps disappear.

I sat in the Beetle for a few minutes, listening to it settle. The engine clicked as it cooled. I didn't take my hands from the steering-wheel. Beetle seats are comfortable, the gear-stick was warm, the air smelt of potato crisps and fizzy lemonade. Condensation began to run down the windows. I traced my fingers in it, an abstract, circular picture with lines across and dots all around. Then I wrote 'hello', took a breath and opened the door.

I breathed deeply. The smell of the sea was strong, as close to perfume as air can be. Salty, almost alcoholic, like a wall you can walk inside. I held my breath and let myself see stars before taking another. The stars I made were red and blue, the ones that speckled the sky were twinkling. I tapped my board and locked the car.

A flight of curving steps, carved out of rock, led up to the hotel entrance. There was a light burning in the porch, and a glass-fronted menu box by the door, but no menu was displayed. A couple of rusty drawing-pins sat at the bottom of the box, and a ball-point pen without a cap. Dark, uncurtained windows stared down at me. I had an overnight bag with me; I pushed the door open with my foot and elbowed my way inside.

There was a bell on the reception desk; I rang it, turned around and leaned back on my elbows. I felt my mother ringing in my head, and all the things I know about her. My heart was beating fast but I was calm. No panic. The soles of my feet tingled but they didn't sing. My nose was hot but not red, and I didn't blink. Some worn leather armchairs were arranged around an empty fireplace, a table with a collection of old magazines stood to one side. A rack of brochures of things to do in Cornwall; a goldfish tank containing five fish, rubber weed and a blue underwater castle. The smell of cooking vegetables wafted from somewhere and feet creaked the floorboards above my head. I turned to ring the bell again, but before I could, as my hand hovered over the pinger, I saw her, I recognised her immediately.

She was the receptionist, and she was plump love on legs, wearing a hair-clip in the shape of a leaping dolphin. She was everything I had imagined, and I reeled. I looked at her as I looked at Supertubes when I first saw that Portuguese wave, as beautiful a thing as you could see in the world, as living as a woman, and you kiss it as you surf. Spume fills the air behind you, warm as a blanket. And there was a dolphin there that watched me.

She had big dark-brown eyes, her face was round and the colour of wheat beer, and her lips were glossy and red. She had small cheeks, like bubbles in simmering caramel. When she smiled she showed white, big teeth, and tilted her head to one side. She wore little blue enamel bird ear-rings, and a blue stoned ring on the little finger of her right hand. She wore a plain white blouse and a short black skirt. Her breasts were big and made the blouse pocket between its pearly buttons so around her waist I could see a tear-shaped inch of her stomach. The skin was fleshy but firm, exactly plump, the same colour as her face. I leaned towards her, my heart climbed into my mouth and began to play a tune on my teeth. It whispered in my ear and dabbed spots of moisture into the corners of my eyes. I looked down her, she looked up me, frowned and said, 'Yeah?'

Her voice was loaded with moans and edged with a grunt. When she frowned, little lines furrowed her forehead, her eyebrows came together and her eyes shrunk. She could not hide her looks, they just changed, as if heavy weather had passed over her. 'Yeah . . .' I said. I'd been thinking about how close my mother could be – six feet, ten, twenty, forty – then I'd lost the thought, now it ran back and tapped me. I smiled. I think I had my mouth open, like cartoon Tom when he sees a female cat. I think tiny red hearts were appearing and popping over my head, and my tongue was hanging down to the floor. I felt moist all over, and this moisture was breeding cream.

'Yeah . . .' I said, again.

'What?'

'Is Mrs Blaine staying here?'

'Mrs Blaine . . .' She looked down and flicked through the pages of the hotel register. Now I could see down her blouse. She was wearing a lacy white bra. There were whorls on the lace, the skin was pinched at her cleavage, and damp. All my creases were sticking together, her skin was smooth, and there was a mole on the rise of her right breast. Smooth as milk, twice as sweet; eight times as sweet, or ten. Looking down at her I felt as I do when a wave begins to break behind me. I'm climbing in the sea and it's roaring behind me. It's fat, warm and deep. I'm thinking so hard about the wave, concentrating on it badly, watching it come, waiting to shift my back foot forward and it comes. But it comes too quickly, almost unexpectedly and as I push up I lose my grip. My foot slips sideways off the board, I'm trying to get it back but it's too late, it's gone, the wave's over me and suddenly I'm full of water. My mouth's full, and my lungs. My leash is twisting around my ankle and the board is flying up and away from me. She stood up straight, and said, 'Sorry. No Mrs Blaine.'

'Are you sure?' I said. I'm praying now, for her and my mother, and I took out the postcard. My hand was boiling. 'She was here.' I passed her the card. It was creased and torn at one corner. Our fingers touched. She had big hands.

She read it and said, 'That looks like Mrs Leaf's writing.'

'Mrs Leaf?' I said.

'Exactly.'

'Is her first name Diana?'

'Yeah.'

'Is she here?'

'I think she's gone for a walk, but she is staying.' She turned the register around on the desk and pointed at the previous week's entries. Mrs Leaf's handwriting was my mother's.

'A walk?' I said. 'At this time of night?'

'Every night since she's been here. She goes to the top of the cliff and back.' She nodded over her shoulder. 'She takes a torch . . .'

'Estelle!' A high and angry voice yelled from a room behind the reception desk.

She raised her eyes to the ceiling and shook her head. 'The old man,' she hissed.

'Oh,' I said.

A bloke appeared. He had a thin, dumb face, with pale grey eyes and small teeth. He stood with his legs apart and his toes pointing out. He was carrying a pen and a clipboard, and looked at his watch. He tapped it, held it to his ear, tapped it again and shook it. I nodded at him, he glared at me, then snarled 'You got those menus done?' at Estelle. She pulled out a drawer, reached in and took out some menus. The old man snatched them, looked at me again, and went back to his room.

'Bastard,' she hissed.

'She takes a torch?'

'Eh?'

'My mother. She takes a torch on her walk?'

'Yeah,' said Estelle, 'sorry.' She looked over her shoulder and scowled. I put the postcard back in my pocket, and instead of walking around the reception desk, putting my arms around her waist and dropping my lips to her neck, untucking her blouse and fingering the tiny rolls of flesh that stacked over her waist like lips, and easing her breasts out, instead of this, I checked in.

Estelle is the sort of name I hoped she would have, the sort of name you give a wave, a hurricane or a type of cloud formation. She offered to carry my bag to my room, but I hate people doing things for me. I won't have it. If I can do it, let me. I could have followed her up the stairs, I could have watched her thighs going before me, and breathed her smell, but I could wait. I am patient, I have faith, taught by water.

I was born in my caul. The midwife shook her head at me, and thought to herself that I wouldn't last long, but she didn't say anything. The membrane was taken away but not incinerated. So I cannot drown, I cannot die by water in any way. I won't fall asleep in the bath, or be overcome by heat in a shower. I don't need to worry about travelling by ferry. In an ancient time I would have been taken from my parents and saved for the priests. The omens were as good for me as they can be. Estelle was bright, she was hot, she was mine from the moment that I realised that her hair-clip was not a sausage, and I was hers before I finished unpacking. I unpacked – I lay my clothes on the bed – opened the windows and stepped on to the balcony. I stared down, leaning on the railing.

The sea was slow and unpredictable, the cliffs were black, the path my mother had taken snaked away to the right, past a bench before climbing steeply to a grassy plateau. Then it took a bend and disappeared out of sight. I fetched a chair and sat down to wait. The sun was setting in pink and yellow slices, fat and light, the clouds moving slowly through the colour like a sea in the sky.

Sunset is a good time to surf. I break rules. I surf alone and I surf in bad light, sometimes even in the dark. I only began surfing in the dark a year ago, but as I did, I wondered why I never had before. When clouds and the night steal day, and you can't see the beach, and you must predict a wave by feeling, sound and instinct, and cat sight, then you become good. The sea is not yours, you belong to it, the trust is mutual. You know how to spell its name and it can spell yours in your blood; I first surfed in the night at Porthleven.

It was September. It had been a cool day; by half past nine it was cold enough to freeze beer. In Kulmbach, in Germany, the strongest beer in the world was first made when a brewery worker forgot to bring some barrels in for the night. In the morning, the brewery boss, furious that the worker had not done his work properly, forced the man to drink the unfrozen liquor at the centre of the barrels. The man took one taste and before he collapsed, declared it the most delicious brew he had ever tasted. It was the colour of dark honey and nearly as thick. It clings to the side of the bottle, and must be sipped, always sipped.

I wore my heaviest wet-suit, mits, boots and a helmet, and paddled into the dark slowly. I know the Porthleven break well, and the reef like the back of my hand. It can be a busy place, also one of the most dangerous places in the world; if you don't know what you're doing, forget it. I was scared – I know that – scared enough to bleed as I took the sets and looked over my shoulder. The beach had disappeared. All I could see was the dark edge of land where it met the sky, house lights in the town and the lights of cars as they drove along the coast road. Some cars have square lights, and others have round; I'd thought about slapping a miner's helmet on my head, but there was no point. I want to illuminate nothing – the point is that I don't want to illuminate the waves, and I don't want to illuminate you. Illumination is one of those double words, and I won't use it again.

I caught a good left-hander. All I could see was its lip, cresting away from me, throwing spray into the dark, roaring gently behind me. The sound was changed by the dark, given a sinister, softer note, as if it was being swallowed. Then it was swallowing itself, the night and the salty smell. I kept low, adjusting my line, and all I could see was that creaming lip, the nose of my board and my feet. When I looked up, the sky could have been the sea, I could have been upside down, I could have been surfing air. If I wiped out then I could have died, I could have been forced to the bottom and ripped open on the reef. I may not drown but I could have my belly split on the vicious rocks that frig the sea at that spot; I did not think about them, I did not think at all. I surfed. It was big water, I was small, my fear increased as the wave slackened and, to my right, slammed against the harbour wall. House lights blinked on the water, I began to shout through the soles of my feet, and I shouted once with my mouth. What I was doing is as dangerous as you can be, foolish and stupid. I could be beaten up by lifeboatmen, and banned from all the breaks in Cornwall by life-guards.

There was a knock on the door. I got up and opened it. Estelle was standing in the corridor with a pile of towels in her arms. She'd taken the dolphin out of her hair so strands of it were hanging down, framing her face. I wanted to pick her up and sit her down on me. 'Sorry,' she said, 'but I don't think you've got one.'

'I brought my own,' I said.

'Have one of these anyway. They're fresh.'

'Thanks.'

She came into the room, and as she passed me, I smelt her. She smelt of clean sheets, pressed tight against my nose, and polish. She draped the towel over the end of the bed, smoothed it down and said, 'She's not back yet.'

'I know.' I pointed to the chair. 'I've been waiting for her.' She stood by the window, looked at the sky, the sea and then down at the car park. She pointed at the Beetle.

'You're a surfer?'

I don't know if she meant it as a question or a statement, but I didn't care. 'Yeah,' I said. 'You ever been?'

'Never.' She looked at me and smiled. I watched the smile build from her lips and her teeth, like when you're a kid and you watch someone paint a picture and you think it's magic. 'And I don't like them,' she said.

'Who's them?'

'Surfers.'

'Nor me,' I said. 'Bunch of tossers . . .'

Estelle squinted. 'Talking about yourself?' She shook her head, made a fist and brushed my arm with a pretend punch. 'That's a bad sign.'

I shook my head. 'I surf, but I do it alone. I don't want anything to do with the macho stuff. Surf's not about what you wear, what tricks you can do, or where you've been . . .'

'Isn't it?'

'No.'

'You could've fooled me . . .'

'You've been talking to the wrong surfers.'

'You're the only one I've ever talked to,' she said. Estelle didn't look at me with contempt, but I waited for it. I waited for her to walk away without another word, but she didn't. Caught between women, and there was a warm, crusty edge to the atmosphere, as if we were standing by an open oven door. She patted the towel on the bed and said, 'So why do you do it?'

'Why does a bird fly?'

'I hate people who answer a question with a question. I think it means that they're insecure or something.'

I like a woman who knows what she hates. It can only be uphill from now on.

'There are two things I do that free me.' I coughed, and tasted kippers in my mouth. 'Surfing's one of them.'

'What's the other?'

Saved by my mother's torch. I saw it out of the corner of my eye, coming down the track. I didn't answer Estelle; I went straight to the window and looked out.

My heart started racing like it goes when I drink two cups of coffee one straight after the other. The torch-beam swung from left to right, and I saw her feet. She was wearing boots, she was walking slowly, picking the way carefully. I stood back from the window and hid myself with the curtain. Estelle stood behind me; 'I'm sorry,' I said, 'but my mother's coming.' She moved forward to look out, but I took her arm and pulled her back. 'Don't let her see you.'

'Why not?'

'I don't want to frighten her off.'

'Frighten her off?'

'Yeah.' I took a step back from the curtain.

'Why would you do that?'

'I haven't seen her for eight years.'

'What?'

'Yeah,' I said. 'Today's an important day for both of us.' As I spoke, Estelle turned away and looked at the floor. She had hot breath. She flicked at some stray hairs and licked her lips.

Now I heard my mother for the first time in eight years. She left the path and crossed the car park. Her boots scraped the gravel, and then she stopped. I didn't look down, but I knew she was looking at the Beetle. My heart was banging hard now, and I was in a night surf sweat, flushing my skin like a shower. It was cold and then it was hot; Estelle said, 'She's in number sixteen, at the end of the corridor. You want me to tell her you're here?'

'No!' I spoke too sharply, too loud. I apologised. 'I'm sorry,' I said, and I touched her for the second time. I felt her skin beneath the material of her blouse. It was plump and firm. Our faces were close, the smell of fresh sheets never left her. I heard the hotel door open and my mother's delicate footsteps around the reception desk. Then on the stairs, into the corridor outside my door, down the corridor, a key in a door, the door opens, she's in.

FOUR

I last saw my mother in October 1984. I was in the kitchen with her, ready for school.

They were desperate days. Dad had been dead a month. Mother and I rarely spoke; when we did, it was only to communicate necessary information, no more.

'Good morning.'

'Goodnight.'

'I'm off.'

'Bye.'

My last sight of her was as she stood in the kitchen, staring out of the window at the back garden. She had let her hair grow the way it wanted to, and some blonde highlights that had been applied before the accident were growing out, so now her natural colour was showing at the roots. She hadn't brushed it in the morning, she was wearing her nightie and dressing-gown.

There were fences between us and the people either side. These fences were six feet tall, flimsy, made of thin wood, but they could have been made of concrete blocks, topped with barbed wire, thirty feet tall, mined either side. While our neighbours lived – by the sound of it – happy lives, we lived in gloom and silence. When Dad had been alive, he had filled the house and garden, he had been friendly with everyone in the street, and everyone had been friendly with him. Nothing phased him, he enjoyed his work. He was the factory manager. The factory made beef pies, beef and vegetable pies, pasties, chicken and mushroom pies, sausage rolls, and was developing a line of fish products. He was responsible for a work-force of one hundred and twenty-five, he believed that management should be seen on the shop floor, he was captain of the factory general knowledge quiz team. He never got drunk, he never came home late, he never raised his voice at me, or hit me.

One day . . . I was going to tell the story of his death, how he died in the factory, but I find it difficult to think about. It was a gruesome accident.

So I left my mother standing over the sink, twirling her fingers in her hair, and went to school. I used school as a means of escape, never something to escape from. A gate to life and that. I had friends there, but after his death, I withdrew into my lessons. At home, after I had done my homework, I either walked to the beach and tried the dead waves Margate blows, or I settled down on my bed with headphones on, listening to music and reading surf mags. Also I designed wicked new boards, and drew perfect barrelling waves, the sort I saw in my dreams. Dreams of waves were the best times in those times. Waves so beautiful, so complete and long, high as buildings but soft as pillows, blue as my Dad's eyes, frothing with all our tears. Kind waves and waves that spoke, kissing lips and impossibly hollow tubes. I dream in colour, sound and smell. I sleep in a foetal ball. My favourite subject at school was Geography, and I was good at it. I have the grades to prove it, and a place at Exeter University. Other people choose Exeter because it's one of the best, but I chose it because it's best for the best waves in the country. I know about commitment, and will not allow my studies to suffer, but I cannot let the sea suffer either. Surfers Against Sewage, The Old Counthouse Warehouse, Wheal Kitty, St Agnes, Cornwall, will not let the sea suffer. They know their stuff, and I wouldn't mind working for them. Geography is about understanding the earth. It was created from gas and dust five hundred million years ago, and is in danger now. To understand what we are doing to it and the peril we are in, you have to understand its whole life, and the parts that make it up. Join now!

Mother was thinner than I had ever seen her, hunched like a snapped insect over the sink. Completely gone in her loss and her inability to absorb the truth. Dad had given her reason, and had been the opposite to her. She wanted his bustle and optimism. She didn't turn to watch me go, the last syllable she spoke to me came softly, creeping like a mouse across the floor. 'Bye.' I'm gone.

Now I'm here, standing outside room sixteen, at the end of the corridor. I can hear her in the room, moving from the bathroom to the bed, rustling her coat off and putting her boots by the wardrobe. My fist is up, held over the door. There's movement behind me; when I turn to look I see Estelle. She looked at me, held my eyes for as long as it took to buzz my root, but she didn't stop walking. She was wearing flat black shoes with rubber soles, and black tights.

The number sixteen on the door was not screwed on straight. The number was pierced by three holes; one of the screws was missing, the other two had been screwed in crooked. I heard a tap being run and a glass chinking on the side of the sink. So close to her, my heart began to flutter, it began to slow, and I knocked.

How close can you be without touching? As close as my mother and I when I saw her last; now she came to the door and opened it, and I saw her again.

What had been brown was grey, and what skin had been smooth was now covered in wrinkles and the shadows of capillaries. She looked like a ghost, she looked like smoke from a dampened fire, my mother. She looked taut but she still looked elegant, controlled. She'd been thin but she was thinner now; as she'd thinned so she appeared to be taller. Her nose and cheeks were lightly dusted with powder, her lips were flat and pale, and her eyes had darkened. I remembered them as blue, but now they were brown. Can this be possible?

'Mother?' I said.

'Duncan,' she said.

She stood back to let me into her room; as I passed her, she touched me gently on the elbow, but we didn't embrace, we didn't kiss. 'Should I have rung?' I said.

'No. I was expecting you,' she said. The voice! Of course! It was precise and quiet, with layers of possibilities. It could be kind and it could admonish, or encourage or coo, all with the slightest changes. The words came slowly, as if she practised them.

'Thanks for the card.'

'Did the hotel stamp it?'

'Yes.'

'I'm sorry,' she said, 'I didn't have the strength to tell you myself. I tried, but I lost.'

'Mother . . .' I said, and I moved towards her. She spread her right hand and pointed to a chair.

'Please sit down.'

I did.

'Would you like something to drink?'

'Thanks.'

'Tea? I'm afraid I haven't got anything stronger.'

'Tea's fine.'

She went to a table and flicked on a kettle. As she moved, she stalked, like a heron or a flamingo, long, steady and elegant movements, each worked out in advance, her eyes looking straight at what she was doing, as if they controlled her hands. She dropped tea-bags in mugs, she licked her lips, she was wearing smart grey trousers and a patterned blue and grey pullover. Her fingers looked like bones. The kettle boiled, she made the tea, I stared out of the window.

'There you are,' she said, and she passed me my mug before sitting opposite me. She crossed her legs, and now the bottom half of her body looked like a relief map of ocean currents, sweeping from – say – the Indian Ocean, through the Arafura Sea to the Pacific. She kept still as she sat, took a sip of her tea, and I stared at her. I think I knew then what was to come, what I should expect, but I threw the awful thought away. Grief comes at its own pace, it doesn't need hurrying. She caught my eye once, then looked away; she caught it again, and had to look away again. She looked as though I scorched her when I looked at her; I got in there with 'It's good to see you again,' a banal thing to say, but each syllable was carrying more emotion than you could stack in a palace. Worse than catching a psycho wave, worse than knowing you've failed. I couldn't look at her when she said, 'I'm sorry.'

Her voice was as thin as she was, quiet as wing-beats. She licked her lips, but it didn't help her.

'How long's it been?' she said.

'Eight years.'

She shook her head and looked straight at me. 'You've changed.'

'Yeah . . .'

'I knew you would have, of course, but looking at you; I wonder if I'd have recognised you in the street.'

'I'd have known you.'

'And your voice,' she said. 'You are your father's son.'

'Of course I am.'

'No; what I mean is . . .' and she looked away, searched the floor for something that wasn't there and looked at me again '. . . some sons are lost, you know? They're drifting between their parents, they don't seem to belong to one or the other. I'm happy for you.' She put her hand out and twitched her fingers towards me. I looked at her nails and the creases on her knuckles. I almost reached out and touched her, but something stopped me. What was the something? The seductive sound of waves beating at the base of the cliffs, the smell of salt in the air or the cry of a luminescent gull as it flashed by the window? She searched my face for something. 'Did you get spots?' she said.

'What do you mean?'

'When I wasn't around. I used to wonder sometimes; what teenage ailments were upsetting you . . .'

'I was alright.' I cleared my throat. 'I survived.'

'Marcus and Susan looked after you?'

'Yes.'

Silence. Wing-beats and cotton.

Piles of fresh towels and milky nipples.

'I am sorry,' she said. 'Do you believe me?'

I nodded, but said nothing.

'Say you do.'

'Mother,' I said, 'I believe you.'

'Really?'

'Please.'

She looked away suddenly, tipped her head and I thought she was going to cry. Her bottom lip began to quiver, but when she looked back at me, her lips were dry. 'When I left,' she said, 'I didn't know what I was doing, but I knew I was lost without your Dad. There was never anyone like him; it was unfair.'

'I know.'

'And I was unfair.'

'No.'

'I was.'

I cleared my throat. 'Where did you go?'

The trace of a smile tapped the corners of her mouth. 'Where didn't I go?'

'I don't know . . .'

'You think you can escape by running, but the pain's in your head, and unless you cut that off, you'll never lose it. And I thought about that . . .'

'What?'

'Cutting it off. I got close . . .'

I wanted to move to her now. I pressed my feet down hard and shifted forward. I imagined a speeding sea behind me, I wanted to lose it and hold her; she noticed my movement and stiffened. She hugged herself around the waist.

'Mother . . .'

'I know.'

'Please . . .'

'No,' she whispered. 'Wait.'

Now, racing towards the feeling of happiness and relief, I felt the beginning of anger in me, growing like a ball grows in size as it approaches you. The ball appears to get smaller to the thrower, and larger to the catcher. Travel with the ball and it's the same size; obvious to anyone, but I had to control myself. It passes happiness, it overtakes relief; I wouldn't shout, but I said, 'Wait? How much longer? And you say you know!'

'Duncan . . .'

'You don't know anything! Do you think I wasn't screwed by Dad's death? Do you think I just carried on, that the surf never changed? Didn't you ever think that I could have been the only person to help you? That we could have seen it through together?'

'Seen it through?' She smiled at these words, but the smile was not a smile anyone would recognise. The corners of her mouth went up and she showed her teeth, but her eyes didn't change, and the muscles in her face didn't relax. 'What do you mean?'

'I don't know, and maybe I don't care any more.' I took a deep breath and air wheezed into me. 'You rejected me for nothing; nothing ever rejected you!'

Blood drained from her face. 'I rejected you? You thought that? You think that?'

'What else could I think?'

'But . . .'

'You even changed your name! Mrs Leaf? For God's sake!' My voice hit a high note that split the back of my nose. 'What the hell was wrong with Blaine?'

'I was overcome.' There were tears in the corners of her eyes. 'I thought I could forget, become anonymous; then I thought I might be happy. I didn't want to take you down with me, and I could have.'

'And you're here now.'

'Yes.'

'And we're arguing,' I said.

'Yes.'

'I never knew what I'd say to you, never exactly. There were always too many questions, and I knew the answers would never be the right ones, even if they were the ones I wanted.'

'What do you mean?' she said. Tears dropped from her cheeks and spotted her blouse.

Now I put down my tea, said, 'I don't know,' and stood up. Everything she had given me I wanted to give to her, and anything to relieve her. The composure and calm, her carefully made-up face, her smart trousers and the little gold brooch on her blouse; her neatly cut hair, her delicate fingers, her correct voice; these things began to crumble in front of me. A piece dropped here, another piece there, and they gathered together in a pile on the floor. One piece leaked and another wept. I went to her. For a second she cringed, then she let herself go, and could not resist.

I knelt on the floor, she put her mug down, and I put my arms around her waist and my head in her lap. I heard her stomach gurgling, she smelt like an autumn meadow after rain. I squeezed her gently, and heard her squeak, as if I was forcing air out of a balloon. She moved her hand, it hovered over my head and then she touched my hair. First she just lay her fingers there, but then she took some strands and began to twirl them. She did this very gently, as if I was a pet and never a son. She whispered my name, I said nothing, she said it again, and laid her other hand on my back. I could feel her skin through my shirt and it was cold. She was trembling slightly, as an injured mouse trembles at a cat, but I did not want to hurt her. I understood her. I knew the answers to the questions I had; I just wanted to hear the answers from her. I wanted her to understand, but I think she did. 'I can't say any more than sorry,' she whispered. 'I know that now.' I believed her, and nodded into her lap. When I opened my eyes, they were full of tears, and I hadn't expected that. I keep my emotions carefully, I keep them in separate boxes, tied with string. I closed my eyes and turned my head so my cheek was resting on the damp I had put on her blouse.

An hour later, we sat in chairs on the balcony. The sea rolled and tossed beneath us, the sound of other hotel guests drifted up from the restaurant. We'd talked generally. Was I still surfing? Was Susan still the most honest woman in the world? Was Marcus the highest earning insurance salesman in the country? Did I ever go back to Margate? Was I looking forward to university? I asked her where she'd been and she told me – she'd lived in Ireland, travelled to America and crossed it from east to west, she'd spent six months in Indonesia, three in India, a year in Africa, another year in Spain and Portugal. All the time she was trying to lose and forget, travelling light and staying in the cheapest hotels. Her only luxury was drink, her only vice was misery. But the further she travelled from it, the closer it shadowed her; 'When I was in Spain, it finally didn't matter any more . . .'

'What didn't?'

She shrugged. 'Anything. Anything beautiful, any happiness I saw, or grief. I was numb, and that's when I knew what I had to do.'

'What was that?'

She looked at me, and I saw the edge of her old eyes in the new. 'I'll tell you.'

'What?'

'I was staying in Gerona, in a room the size of a wardrobe, high in a house that backed on to a street of prostitutes. I could lean out of the window and watch a madam tap her feet, sing snatches of song and shout at her girls, while the girls leered at men, and the men put their hands in their pockets and rattled their change. There was also this family of cats in the street; the kittens used to wail all the time. And there was a cathedral behind the house, and another church below. At midnight, the cathedral bells would strike twelve; on the eleventh strike, the other church would begin to strike. I'd stick moist tissue in my ears, but I couldn't sleep.

'When I wasn't trying to sleep, I used to sit in cafés, drinking wine and watching the world go by. I remember a man approaching me and asking for a cigarette. He was wearing a straw hat and carried a large stick and three bulging plastic bags. He had this long face; I gave him a cigarette, and then he sat on a bench, took out some staved paper, and began composing music. He conducted with one hand and whistled as he wrote. He was a beggar but I envied him; he had his bags and he had his music, and I felt useless. What did I have?'

'Me?'

'You. I know,' she said. 'I thought about you in the

cathedral. I gate-crashed a wedding in the chapel there; I sat with the groom's party, at the back. Behind me, a man sat at a little organ, and another man sat with a violin on his knees. The priest was fat and moved slowly. After rings were exchanged and the blessing had been given, the principals moved behind the altar and signed a register. Arc lights were moved from one position to another so a pair of photographers could take their pictures, and as the groom put pen to paper, the priest coughed, the organist looked up, nudged the violinist and they started to play the most beautiful tune. The music rose to the ceiling and hung there; I listened to the end, then stood and left the chapel, and made my way to the cathedral doors. The rest of the party followed, and while they waited in the sunshine for the happy couple, everyone lit cigarettes. Children were armed with bags of rice, clouds of smoke rose into the sky, women kissed and men slapped each other on the back. Then the groom appeared, followed by the bride, who stepped, squinting into the sunshine. She was wearing a cream dress with patterns of pearls on the sleeves and front, and carried a bouquet of roses. Everyone was happy, and I thought then that I would never, ever be happy again. And I realised that trying to escape had only imprisoned me; I finished my travels the next day, and I knew what I had to do.'

'What was that?'

'Guess.'

'No.'

Now my mother began to cry. Tears filled her eyes and began to flood her cheeks. She heaved with effort, I passed her a handkerchief, she took it and held it to her face. 'I was in London, dead as a living thing can be, so I decided to do the thing properly.' She blew her nose. 'I decided to throw myself under a train. I thought it would be the easiest way to do it, that there'd be no chance of surviving. I didn't want to make a mistake, to have people think it was just a cry for help.

'So I went to Clapham Junction. The platform was busy but not crowded. It was easy to find a place to be alone. I stood near the edge and looked at the tracks. I thought about you. I thought about you and I thought about Dad, I remembered the holidays we had together. Every one, one after another, and little things that happened to us. You remember the first board you had?'

'The one Dad made?'

'Yes.'

'How could I forget it?'

'Have you still got it?'

'Yes.'

'Does it still work?'

'I should think so.'

Mother nodded her head. There was a sudden still in the air, a pause as long as sleep. She took a deep breath, held it, blew and said, 'And I thought about my miscarriage.'

'What miscarriage?'

'I had one, a couple of years after you were born . . .'

'Oh God.'

'You could have had a sister,' she said.

'No . . .'

'I always wanted a daughter; I was five months gone when I lost her . . .'

'I never knew.'

'You were never told.'

'Why not?'

'Why don't parents tell their children things? I don't know.'

I could have had a sister. 'So?'

'So what?'

'So you're at Clapham Junction . . .' I said.

'And I was going to die. I was there,' she said, 'absolutely convinced. All the thoughts and the meaning behind every one; how could I have been so stupid?'

'Were you?'

'Yes. I see that now, but only because of Clive. Have I told you about him?'

'You know you haven't.'

'He was there. He'd watched me. He knew what I was going to do, he knew the Express was coming before I did. I was staring at the sky, the station had dissolved around me, like ice in a warm drink, and all I had to do was sink in the drink, swallow it as I went down, and all the pain would go away. I'm sorry; I don't mean to sound self-pitying, but it's how I felt, what I felt. For a moment I was absolutely free, as sure about what I was doing as I'd ever been. I heard the station announcer say something, but I couldn't work out what he meant. It was a babble of names, stations, apologies for lateness, but all the words were strung together, they banged around inside my head; I remember, I put my hands to my ears, I felt my mouth fill up with salt and my mind teemed with voices and memories. Our holidays. Do you remember them?'

'How could I forget?' I said.

'They were the happiest times of my life.'

'And mine.'

'Holidays,' she said again, holding the word like I can hold a wave, hidden from all the surfers who crowd the beach they think they own. 'I was standing at the edge of the platform, and I had this voice in my head, whispering at an echo of your father's voice. Do you remember his voice, Duncan?'

'Yes,' I said. 'And his whistling.'

'Oh yes,' she said weakly. 'Gershwin, wasn't it?'

'Yeah.'

'Couldn't he whistle the whole of *Porgy and Bess*?'

'That's what he used to say.'

Her smile was thin and tight, like a crinkled leaf had grown on her face, and was opening up for me. 'I don't think he could.'

'Nor do I,' I said.

'Not a whole three hours of music.'

'Maybe he meant that he could whistle along with it.'

Mother nodded, staring at me, and then blinked. The blink took her back to Clapham Junction, and the train that came hurtling down the line towards her. A train with innocent passengers sitting in their seats, people sleeping, reading, talking, sniffing, writing, dreaming. She said, 'A whole three hours . . .'

'Yeah,' I said.

'That music; as it filled my head it fixed me to the spot. I couldn't move though I wanted to. There was nothing I wanted more; I had to force it out of my head. I leaned forward, I could see the train as it came around the bend towards the station, so then I closed my eyes, took a couple of steps towards the edge and Clive grabbed me, pulled me back and stood between the train and what I'd planned. I still tried to throw myself forward, but he's a big man. He's big in every way . . .'

'I'm sure he is.' I spoke to the floor.

'Duncan . . .'

'What?'

'He saved my life.'

'He must be special.' I didn't look up.

'He is.'

'Am I?' I looked at her.

'Are you what?' she said.

'Special?'

'Of course you are.'

'As him?'

'You,' she said, 'are a different kind of special. You give me a link, memories, the past, but he gives me the future. Hope.'

I know I'm jealous, but it's not just for myself, but for Dad. I should have saved Mother's life, I should have been allowed to watch her. I said, 'I suppose he persuaded you to let me know you were here.'

'No. That was my decision.'

'Why?'

'Why do you think?'

'Because you love me?'

'Yes . . .' she said.

'And?'

'How can I tell you?'

'Just say it . . .'

'What's the point?'

'The point is, Mother, that I'm your son. I never spent a day without wondering where you were, what had happened to you, what was happening to you.'

'I never spent a day not thinking the same about you.'

'And now we're together again.'

'Yes,' she said, 'we are.'

'And you're going to tell me why. Why, after all this time . . .'

'I don't think I can.'

'Why not?'

'Because whatever I say would never be enough for you.'

'I don't understand,' I said.

'I was sick, Duncan, I know that now. Melancholia was my child . . .'

'I'm your child.' My voice was up.

'Then it's your brother.'

'Melancholia?'

'And not just that. Something deeper, a thing I was born with, and God knows what that was. And who wants to know, anyway?'

'I do.'

'What good would that do you?'

'The knowledge that it might do you good.'

'That's the sort of thing Clive would say . . .'

'Is it?'

'Duncan. I had to see you again because I wanted to say goodbye, and properly this time.'

My ears blew. My tongue felt as though it was red-hot, I opened my mouth, but only made a whining sound.

'Duncan?'

'Wheeeeee . . .'

'Duncan!'

'Goodbye?'

'Yes.'

'Goodbye?'

'Duncan . . .' She put her hand out to me, but I moved from it.

'Where are you going now?'

'Away.'

'But where?' She turned away from me, I raised my voice. 'Mother! This is crazy! I find you after all this time, only to have you tell me that you're going away again.'

'I knew you wouldn't understand.'

'It's not a question of understanding.'

'Isn't it?' She knew it wasn't. You could tell.

'No.'

'Honestly, Duncan, I can't change my mind, and I won't have it changed.' She pushed her head back and spoke firmly. 'Clive and I are going to Canada.'

'Canada?'

'It's a beautiful country.' That's a fact.

'When?'

'Monday.'

It was Tuesday evening.

'Next Monday.'

'Fuck.'

'Duncan!'

'Fuck, Mother.'

'Don't use that word!'

'Fuck,' I said. 'Fuck, fuck.'

'I know you're upset . . .'

'Upset? Is that what you call it?'

'I love him . . .'

'I love you . . .'

'I love you, but . . .'

'If there's one thing I'd give everything up for, it's you. Anything, Mother. But some, some . . .'

'Duncan!' Now her voice was up, and she had some strength. 'You don't know anything about him so don't jump to conclusions.'

'Will I ever?'

'What?'

'Know anything about him?'

'Maybe. He's coming tomorrow.'

'Here?'

'Yes.'

'To stay?'

'Of course.'

I took a deep breath and said 'OK,' but I was tipping. I was being pushed and I was sweating. I tried to focus on a memory of some wave, but none came. All I thought was that I should have been the one. I should be my mother's son.

FIVE

I went to my room, had a shave, a shower, brushed my teeth and calmed myself by watching the late night weather forecast. The Atlantic chart showed a configuration of lows that would produce the best waves Porthleven can offer. Mother. Isobars and fronts, pressure and windspeeds in black, red and blue; it was beautiful, almost perfect. The forecaster was excited, and had covered the map of the British Isles with more symbols than were necessary. He pointed to the west coast and his glasses almost fell off. When the storm had passed, the swell would run strong and heavy, the highest tides of the month would occur, clear, bright skies would return; all within the week.

I turned the telly off, tossed my towel across the room, lay back in the dark and thought about Estelle.

I had her standing in front of me. A candle was burning in the room, and a fire flickering in the grate. She was wearing a black dress and I was in a black shirt and blue shorts. Her hair was wet, my hair was wet, I carried a towel in one hand, and a drink for her in the other. A spark flew from the fireplace; she jumped back and I jumped forward to sweep it back into the grate.

We touched. She was boiling hot; I bent down to make sure the ember was safe, and as I looked up at her, she looked down. She pursed her lips and I saw the tip of her tongue; she ran it over her teeth, and they glistened and bubbled with saliva.

Her body rose like a kite above me, and when I tugged her string, she flipped slowly in the air. My nose was inches from her legs. I kissed one, then the other. Her hair was down, she tipped her head back, reached up and slipped her dress off her shoulders. She was wearing nothing underneath; I had a glimpse of her naked body, and then the dress was off and over me.

As I struggled to free myself from it, she moved across the room and lay on a purple couch. When I could see again, she was looking at me, her eyes reflected the candle-light, her hair covered one nipple but not the other. Her legs were together, one hand was resting on her stomach, the other stretched out over her head, rubbing the back of the couch. I stood up, and began to unbutton my shirt.

The buttons were awkward, and the last one came off in my hand. The fire was warm on my back. I walked slowly towards her; suddenly she put out her hand and pulled at my shorts.

They ripped, she moved over, pulling all the time, the sound of tearing cotton, the smell of sweat and wine, our noses were touching, she ran her tongue over her teeth again, cupped her breasts in her hands and pushed them towards me. They were glossy and brown. That was enough.

The sea didn't stop, and nor did the hotel. It creaked and moaned through the night, and as I moved to the edge of sleep, it was easy to forget where I was, and easy to imagine I was in a sailing ship, breaking through a heaving, empty ocean. I could hear the rigging whine and strain, the decks creak and the hull shout as it took the regular blows from huge, belligerent waves. Waves that climb from the bottom of the ocean to the top, and from one side to the other, with any power you could name, from the doldrums to a hurricane. Blue waves, grey or green, waves with voices and waves with sight. Waves that carried the grinning skulls of a million dead sailors, a million dead sailors all whispering. Waves the size of houses, and waves that will take my board and fold it into an impossible shape. Waves with names and waves with no names at all; they crashed around me and then I was asleep.

Calm, blue sleep. I wasn't bothered, not by dreams of flying, or of finding myself naked in a public place. All I was was like this: I was in Portugal, I was repeating the greatest days of my life, when other people didn't even go near the water, but I was in it. When Supertubes was as angry as she can be, as unpredictable, angry, deaf.

First thing in the morning, I went for a walk. I left the hotel at half past six. Estelle's father was listening to the radio in the office behind the reception desk. He looked over his glasses at me but didn't say a word. His eyes followed me, he sniffed and tapped his desk with a pen. He looked cross and bored, and hadn't shaved. I nodded to him but he didn't nod back.

I checked the board on the Beetle. It was covered in dew; I wiped some off and tapped the Hot Tuna decal, and for a moment I changed my mind. I wouldn't go for a walk, I'd surf instead. Then I changed back again. If I surfed, I'd be gone all day and I'd forget what I was supposed to be doing.

I took the path I'd seen my mother on. When I reached the grassy plateau, I turned and looked back at the hotel. Apart from mine, all the upstairs curtains were closed; then, as I looked, another pair opened, at the far end of the building. I saw Estelle, and she was wearing a white night-shirt with a picture of the sun rising over palm trees on the front. She stretched her arms over her head, each holding the top of a curtain. I kept still, she looked straight ahead, away from me, towards the sea. Then the arms came down, she ran her hands through her hair, turned around, lifted the shirt over her head, shook it out, threw it on to the bed and disappeared into the room.

I saw her naked back for two seconds, I saw her fleshy waist and her thighs, then they were gone, and I turned around, around the corner and on to the cliff path.

Here, at this place, there was no sign of people at all; the nearest house was a mile away. The next hotel was in St Ives. The path was worn but narrow, and puddled here and there with pools of salt water. All other visitors had gone home. Late September in Cornwall is the best time for the place; surf, empty cliffs, dead vegetation, the evening skies. I was followed by mature sea-birds as I walked; they dived and whirled over me, screeching madly. If I was superstitious, I would have taken some meaning from them, I would have recognised that their cries were stolen from battered and drowned men, men whose bodies had been smashed against rocks, or crushed by the waves that rolled miles before beating on to the secret beaches below. If I was the sort who could take a sight, imagine what that sight smelt like and then smell it; if I could do that, what would I smell now?

Estelle.

The smell of her, fresh from bed. What is that smell? Talc and cotton, cotton and oranges? Hay and salt? What are the tiny noises her body makes as it wakes up? Little squeaks from her creases and pops from her stomach? Estelle. Do you wash your face first, or your teeth? What colour is your toothbrush? I left the path and headed for a stone wall that crossed a summit above.

A low curtain of cloud hung across the eastern horizon; as I climbed, the sun appeared above it and began to warm the sky. Dying bracken rustled in the breeze and filled the air with a rank and cheesy smell. I had been to a place like this before, in 1980. A holiday my mother would remember; a week in Bude at the end of another summer, not hot but warm, and the crowds had gone home.

We stayed in a guest-house ran by a woman – Mrs Henley – who kept cats. Wherever you went you found a cat; sit down in a comfy chair in the lounge and a cat exploded from behind the cushion, get into bed and there was another under the duvet. Mrs Henley called the animals her children, and fed then on prime cuts of fresh fish, carefully diced into china bowls. There was Shandy, Raymondo, Bob, Licorice, Vanilla and George. If you raised your voice at them you were out; if you tried to stroke them your hand would be ripped to shreds. It was cats and it was the smell of the lard Mrs Henley cooked with. She left pots of the stuff cooling on every flat surface, some with cat's hair embedded, others with cat footprints. Lard in the dining room, lard on the stairs and lard drifting into the bedrooms. I had a room of my own. It had a view of the sea, a beach, a row of chalets and a café. I remember the weather: there was no wind, no swell, no rain, the bracken and the grass was bright green to the end of September. I took my board to the beach for the first two days, but it was useless, I could do nothing with it. Better to walk, better to try and find a place where the wind was and we could clear our heads of whatever was clogging them, of whatever had to be blown away.

I remember an evening sitting in the front room, and Mrs Henley came in, wiping her hands on a tea-towel. She nodded at me and started talking about babies; she told Mother that when she was expecting her second child, she developed complications and was taken to hospital by her sister. As she was lying in out-patients, a doctor approached and asked her, 'Where are you bleeding from?' 'I'm from bleeding Bude,' said Mrs Henley, 'and I'd like a bleeding curtain round me.' She laughed like a drain at her story, and I laughed too. I think she told the story as a test; people who didn't laugh were told that there were no vacancies, and denied the pleasure of sleeping in a bed so tall that you were closer to the ceiling than the floor. I remember waking up on my first night, and when I sat up I had the feeling that I was sleeping upside down, and that the laws of gravity no longer applied. Six inches from my face, paint peeled and water pipes gurgled; I lay down again, but could not sleep.

Mrs Henley served breakfast in the front parlour. We had a table by the window, overlooklng the street and a grassy area that led down to the beach. When we were there, there was a souvenir salesman at the next table, who used to catch Dad in conversation. Dad was never at his best in the morning, but was too polite to ignore the man, who would display his samples at the least excuse. Ashtrays, pen-holders, pencils, mugs, china bells, glass monkeys and fat cats, all with spaces where a name could be printed. 'Jersey, Malaga, Rimini, Corfu, Bridlington; you name it,' he said, 'we've done it.' He ate his Cornflakes quickly, talking between mouthfuls. 'Bude's good. Ashtrays go a bomb, and fancy seagulls.' Dad smiled and nodded, and I remember Mrs Henley coming in, and putting plates of bacon in front of us. 'Don't mind Mr Jenkins,' she said. 'He comes every year, but he always leaves, don't you?' 'Certainly do, Mrs Henley,' he said.

There was a butcher's shop in the main street where a pig's head was displayed in the window, with grapes in its eye sockets, an orange in its mouth, a necklace of plums and a line of raisins that ran from the tip of its snout to the middle of its forehead. It was surrounded by other parts of its body: a plate of liver, sliced like leaves, some kidneys, two circles of chops and circles of bacon, like blossoming flowers. The four trotters formed a star in front of the head, and the four leg joints stood upright on the four corners of the slab. The whole was lit by a pink lamp with a fringed shade; it was a small window but the effect was startling. It started to rain, but Dad stood there and shook his head in admiration. 'A work of art,' he said. 'That butcher knows his stuff.' I remember this, I can hear his voice now, clear as a bell. It was quiet and respectful as he looked at the remains of that pig, like a breeze whispering to the sound of running water. The things you remember from when you were a child: why does your brain choose one and forget another? Meat and my father walked hand in hand to every Gershwin concert he could afford.

Another evening, Mrs Henley came into the sitting room with a bottle of sherry, poured a glass for all her guests, and told us the story of Mr Henley's greyhound, Ivan the Terrible. Ivan was entered for a race against his arch rival, Smith's Red Patch. It was the first meeting of the new season; the previous had seen the two dogs competing neck and neck in every race. Patch had taken the championship from Ivan, who had held it for two years running. The dogs were old now, well past their best, but their owners had something to prove. Mr Henley drove to the track early, but as he let Ivan out of the car, disaster struck. The dog caught his tail in the door, severing the tip. Mr Henley took a handkerchief and tied it around the wound; other competitors began to arrive, then Smith and Red Patch. But Patch was injured too. In the close season, his eyesight had faded, and the previous week he had run into a telegraph pole. He wore twelve stitches and an enormous bandage that ran under his jaw and over his forehead; he looked like a cartoon patient. But pride was at stake, the race had to be run, the dogs were put in the traps, the hare ran, the traps opened, six dogs shot out, but Ivan and Patch didn't bother. After a minute, they stepped out and began sniffing each other's wounds, Ivan wagging his tail so hard that the bandage flew off and sailed into the crowd. Mr Henley never raced a dog again, and died in front of a television. 'That television,' said Mrs Henley pointing at the one in the front room. Mother and Dad were laughing, holding hands, wiping their eyes. I remember; happy holidays, relaxed and no worries. Mrs Henley, frayed carpets on the stairs, and cats in the beds.

Would my mother remember? When I say remember, I

mean this: not the simple memories, the time spent, the views, the stories and the food we ate in lard-bucket house, but the feelings. The feelings I had for her, and Dad's too. I needed her. I was hers, more hers than any other person could ever be. At my birth, I had tried to hold on to her for longer than is natural; born in a shroud, born on a cold day. Now, after having no choice, I had to make one. You do not choose your mother, and when you're a child you have no power to keep her with you; I chose to keep her with me now. I could not let another man take her to a cold country; whatever he could offer, I would give. Those old, good memories could be remade, and I was the one with the plan. What plan was this? Nothing that could be written down, but it was there.

Estelle was behind the reception when I walked in. The smell of fried bacon hung in the air. 'Early bird,' she said. She was wearing a low-cut cream blouse with a big bow on the front and a flared black skirt.

'It's going to be a nice day,' I said.

'Bit of a weatherman, are you?'

'You don't need a weatherman to know which way the wind blows,' I said.

'Smart arse,' she said.

'Want to test me?'

'Depends.'

'On what?' I said.

'How I'm feeling.' She reached up and brushed an imaginary speck off her front.

'When do you knock off?'

'I don't.'

'Yes you do.'

She stuck a pencil in her mouth, pulled it out slowly and said, 'How do you know?'

'I'm guessing,' I said. The end of the pencil glistened with spit. I couldn't keep my eyes off it.

'And what are you saying?' She looked at the pencil.

'Fancy a drink later?'

'Might do.'

I tapped the top of the reception desk with my fingers. She watched my fingers, and when I took them away, she rubbed the spot where I had tapped. 'Go on,' I said.

'You buying?'

'Might do,' I said.

She laughed, I laughed and went to have my breakfast.

My mother was sitting at a table by the window. She was drinking a cup of tea. When Estelle's mother began to direct me to a table by the kitchen door, I told her that I'd be sitting with my mother. 'Of course,' she said, and she slapped her forehead. She acted as though she could have done better in life, had wanted to do better but been plotted against. 'Estelle told me.' That name slapped me on the arse. 'Tea or coffee?'

'Tea, please, and some toast and marmalade.'

'Nothing cooked? Sausage and an egg?'

'No thanks.'

Revived by sleep and a shower, my mother looked fresh and cool, though there was a ghostly sheen to her skin, and a resigned, final look in her eyes. She'd put some mascara on, and balm on her lips. Her hair was damp and smelt of flour. As I approached, she stood up, put her hand on my shoulder and kissed my cheek. Peach lip-balm; it was sticky, and left a smear on my skin. I didn't wipe it, I sat down and smiled at her.

'Enjoy your walk?' she said. There was a peculiar edge to her voice, as if she wanted to give it to someone else.

'Yes.'

'Where did you go?'

I pointed out of the window. 'Up there, not far. I sat down

for half an hour, thought about things.'

'That's good.'

'Things I want to tell you.' I cleared my throat. 'Things I want to ask you, find out . . .'

'Sounds serious.'

'I am.'

'Oh dear,' she said.

'Not really . . .'

My tea came.

'What things?' she said.

I poured. 'I don't want to tell you here; after breakfast, maybe we could have a talk.'

'I've got to go to town,' she said.

'St Ives?'

'Yes. We could talk in the car.'

'OK.'

Marmalade is one of the greatest things that comes in a jar. I like it very bitter, dark and heavy on pieces of slim rind; the River Cove Hotel anticipated my desires perfectly. From my mother being there to the view from my window, to plump love on legs, from the sound of the sea in every room, to the marmalade. I would like to take marmalade like the sort I had there and rub it carefully into a number of Estelle's crevices. The one here and the one there, the ones you mention and the ones you don't, and the ones that count up to seven when you're pissed. Then I would like to lick and suck it out, I would not leave a trace of it. I would work carefully, I wouldn't leave her sticky, damp or uncomfortable. No smear and no tears. I would select choice curves of rind and place them in circles around her nipples, and spot their tips with a drop of butter. I would wait for the butter to melt, pick the rind off with my teeth, sooth her skin with some yoghurt if I had any. I would let the yoghurt run slowly over her skin, I'd let some of it soak in and then I'd smear it around with my fingers; I spread my toast and looked across at my mother.

I think I understood her, but I was wrong. She had been boiling with worry as she waited for me; that cleared, to be replaced by this one: how is Duncan going to react to Clive? Who knows? All I knew was that I wanted to be with her. We could find a place in Exeter, a flat at the top of an old Victorian terraced house, with a view over roofs to the hills beyond. As I ate my toast and marmalade and drank a second cup of tea, I did not see that my arse was running ahead of my head, or that my head was too big. You miss what's under your nose, and all your nose does is run.

SIX

My mother had a shopping list. She folded it neatly and put it in her purse, stood in front of a mirror in reception and brushed her hair. She took out a powder compact and dabbed at her nose, she made a cat's arse with her lips, licked a finger and adjusted some smudged mascara, and then she was ready to go.

Estelle was still behind the desk. A couple were checking out, and as she totalled their bill, she looked up to watch me pass. She kept her pen to the paper, she followed me with her eyes. I narrowed mine at her, and smiled. My mother was through the door, holding it open for me, waiting. I had these fast spurts of blood going off in my legs, and a tapping in my head. The more I saw Estelle the more I knew. The more I thought about my mother the more I bled. When I thought about the perfect configuration of lows in the Atlantic, and the swells already building east of Bermuda, the more I left the soles of my feet pleading to sing. So much love. Too much sex. Enough sex to build a town, all pumping into the sky. Struck to the tingling root, turning in hairy circles and back again.

'I think that girl's got eyes for you,' said my mother.

'Which one?'

'Ha,' she laughed. 'Which one . . .'

'Estelle?' I said.

'That's a pretty name.'

'Yeah.'

My mother drove slowly, and said, 'What are you going to tell me, Duncan?'

You get these ideas, and then they will not come out of your mouth. They hold on to your tongue and pull it back, they clamp your teeth and weld it with salt and loss. You have to force them, screaming and fighting, clawing at anything that will hold them. I said, 'What time's he coming?'

'Clive?'

'Yeah.'

'Late afternoon. That's all he could say; it depends on what time he can get away. Why?'

'I wanted to know how much time we've got,' I said.

'We've got all the time in the world, Duncan.'

'No we haven't! We've got half a day on our own, then four days with him around. That's no time at all!'

'I'm sorry you see it that way.'

'How else am I meant to see it? After the weekend, when will I see you again?'

She concentrated on a bend in the road, through a village with grey houses, old men sitting on benches by a graveyard, a neglected vegetable garden and two caravans standing in a field of nettles. A dog jumped off a wall and chased the car for half a minute, then gave up and sloped back the way it had come. 'You can come and stay any time.'

'How?'

I watched her head work. She was going to tell me that I could get on a plane and be there in eight hours, but she knew I couldn't afford to. Then she thought about offering to pay, but she could only do that once every two years.

'What does he do?' I said.

'He's a doctor.'

A doctor. 'What sort of doctor?'

'He's a heart surgeon.'

I said, 'Oh.'

'Oh?'

'What?'

'What's "oh?" meant to mean?'

'Nothing.'

'What did you expect him to be?' She began to drum the top of the steering-wheel with her fingers. 'What did you want him to do?'

I didn't know. 'I don't know.'

'I don't know what sort of person you expected him to be,' she said, 'but I know you'll like him. Nobody doesn't.'

What more can you say, Mother? 'Sure,' I said, and now I'm confused. The good son thinks he is the one his mother needs, and the good son knows that the man his mother wants is someone else. Someone he has never met, but someone who's a saint. I'm not convinced, but I have to control myself.

We drove to St Ives, and arranged to meet in a pub for lunch. I showed a happy face, and was gone.

I was gone for myself, and I was gone for Dad. Maybe I was using him as an excuse, maybe he would have wanted Mother to find another man, but I didn't think so then. I imagined him (minus his fingers) spinning in his grave, cursing doctors over and over again. I could not see him smiling benignly, in exactly the way when he was alive, smiling at my mother as she kissed Clive. What sort of name is Clive? It's sharp and it's empty, there's nothing to it. It finishes before you say it. Jealousy is a fat word, but what I felt was not jealousy. Nor was it hate. Short word. Or envy. Short again. Think of the word 'ice' and that's what I felt. When I heard his name, splinters of ice crept through my body, up my legs and arms, they collected in my neck and then burst into my head. I know I was bad but I couldn't help it. The time I waited for her had built up in me, and the time wore heated clothes and rode a motorbike. I never wanted to hurt my mother, I know what she went through. Compared to her, surfing was nothing. But surfing is exactly what it is, and that is the purest touch with nature. You are between the two liveliest elements, your feet sing and your toes see, you are threatened but absolutely safe. In the morning or the night, it doesn't matter when.

I had no shopping to do, but I went into a surf shop and stared at the stuff. I have two good wet-suits, mits, boots and a helmet, three leashes and two boards. I've got a Surfers Against Sewage sweatshirt, and a Hot Tuna cap (grey denim, big pink Hot Tuna, yellow lettering) and once I had a Crucial T-shirt with an enormous barrel on the back and the words 'Green Room' written beneath, but when I got it home I found it was torn. So I took it back to the shop and got my money back. So when I was in St Ives, I wasn't in buying mode.

What I do like about a surf shop is the potential, the thought that someone has been in, and has been pushed over the edge. He's seen waves, he's stood on a broad and shelving beach and watched waves tumbling towards him, and he's wondered what it would be like to ride them. He's wandered into the shop, is overwhelmed by the colours, the wild splashes that decorate the shirts and shorts, the racks of boards and suits, but he knows these things are not a passport to some secret knowledge. No secret knowledge comes from things, it only comes from doing. He's been in this St Ives shop, this person, but he's never been back. He's bought what he needed and gone. At this moment he's riding the freezing tubes of Thurso, or the cathedrals of Hawaii's northern shores. As I ran my hands up the perfect rails of a fresh Hot Tuna, and moved past the racks of sweats and shorts, the owner of the shop came up to me and said, 'Can I help you, son?'

Oh God. If there's one thing I can't stand, one thing that makes sweat creep over the palms of my hands, one thing that makes my eyes pop and my ears see, it's being called 'son'. I don't mind 'mate', 'ducks', 'darling', 'big boy', 'small boy', 'spaghetti legs', but 'son' hits me. As the word popped out of his mouth, I felt this ball of anger form in my stomach, a raging, steaming thing that attacked my gut and left it in ribbons. I felt my face redden, my cheeks began to sing, I licked my lips and said softly, 'I'm not your son.'

'Sorry?'

'I'm not your son,' I said, harder now.

'I know, but I didn't mean it literal, son.'

Now I yelled, 'I'm not your fucking son, so don't call me that!'

'Hey!' He took a step back, and scratched his chin. 'There's no need to be so touchy . . .'

'There's every need,' I said, taking deep breaths to calm myself, gripping the top of a rack of shorts, looking at my knuckles, which were turning white.

'OK,' he went, holding up his hands, and he backed off. 'Sorry . . .'

'It's easy to say that.'

'Look . . .' he said, and I got the feeling that he didn't know what he was up against, who I was, or what I might do, '. . . I don't want any trouble.'

'Who said anything about trouble?'

'Not me.'

'So don't call me "son" again.'

'I won't.'

'Good.'

Good. I took another deep breath and he did too, and then I left the shop. When I was outside I closed my eyes for a moment, then walked down to the harbour. I touched my forehead; I was hot. I struggled with my memories, my brain and surf. St Ives Bay can produce willing waves, but dangerous rips and currents can screw a good day; Gwenvor and Sennen Cove are only half an hour away; Porthleven a little further, Newquay about the same distance; the town is best for its harbour and the flakes who live there. There are a lot of them; they can be seen in the streets talking about what they are doing, where they've been and their plans for the future. Mainly nothing, nothing and nothing; I could be cruel but I'm not an animal, I'm a human being.

The only person I ever surfed with was Adam, and he would drive from London to catch a wave, then drive back after three hours in the surf because he had to be back at work in the morning. He was a man who knew his breaks, his moves and the technicalities of a long-range weather forecast. He swore that he heard French music in waves, and surfed to listen for it.

One day he told me that he had been in his front garden, and two boys had gone by. One had said to the other 'Are you a human being?' and the other, after a moment's thought, had said, 'Na, course not.'

Adam never had to wax his board, the soles of his feet were like sandpaper. He drove a Golf and liked Messiaen. We didn't spend long together, but he stays in my mind as a surfer who surfed for the right reasons.

What are the right reasons? Your reasons are the right reasons, only then are they right. However, my right reasons are not your right reasons, because right reasons are subjective things, so there's no point me telling you what they are.

Adam is also the only person who ever wrote me a letter about some surf. He had been in Ireland, at Easky, where the tubes are so long and straight that they could be made of steel. He told me it was raining all the time, and that he'd seen a woman in a bar, tall and pale, with black eyes. He had watched her all evening, and she had looked at him once. The one look was enough. He was in prison. He could not get out, she pursed her lips at him, and they were like bars for him.

Her skin was the colour of frost, and her hair like a shadow's shadow. He had to steady himself on the bar; he ordered another drink and asked the barman who she was.

'Who's that?' said the barman.

'Yes.'

'Who?'

Adam pointed. The room was full, he could have pointed at anyone in it, but the finger would have really pointed at her. She drank alone, and listened to a group who were playing in the corner. A man with a beard sang 'Nothing but a child'.

'That's Mary.'

'Mary?'

'She is.'

'Thanks,' said Adam.

'But she doesn't come here too often.'

'Why not?'

'She makes the floor too sticky.'

Adam laughed about this later, but he couldn't in the letter. This woman did not like men. He got no closer to her than twelve feet. He surfs because he trusts the sea and the trust is returned with respect, which is, in its own time, returned. He rides a long board – a Malibu – in the old style. More erect, floating in his movements, slower and quieter. I have always been a rip-and-slash boy, but I see that the old style is more natural. I have to get something out of my system, Adam had done that already. Yes, he used to rip and slash too, but when he got married he changed.

I went to meet my mother in a café on the front. She was there before me; as I approached the place, I saw her through the window. She had a cup of tea on the table in front of her, and was staring through the window. She was holding her head in her hands, and had an old face on her. A face from a holiday she didn't enjoy, or from some time in Margate when she knew she was missing something. All the new confidence and composure had gone. Melancholia is my brother, though I have not met him. I've seen him, he stayed with me, but he never told me who he was. He was the monster under the bed, living with the suitcases and dust, seeing with his fingers. When I sat down opposite her, she looked at me with the old look, then snapped into the new.

'Something the matter?' I said.

'No.' She spoke sharply, then said, 'I'm sorry.' Then quietly, 'Nothing.'

'Sure?' I ordered two more teas.

'Thinking, that's all.'

'What about?'

She fixed me with her eyes. 'I know,' she said. 'I know what you're going through. What you must be thinking.'

I didn't argue.

'It must be awful for you. At least I knew you were alive. I knew where you were, and how you were getting on. Susan always wrote very detailed letters . . .'

'She wrote to you?'

'Didn't she tell you?'

'No.'

'I suppose,' said my mother, 'that telling you what I did was enough for her. I put a big burden on her shoulders; I never doubted that she wouldn't be able to look after you, but I worried that she'd tell you where I was before I was ready . . .'

'No fear of that,' I said. 'Susan's not the telling type.'

'Except when you ask her to be.'

'Except then,' I agreed.

The teas arrived. Mother picked up hers and blew on it, then took a small sip. She looked at me through a cloud of steam, and tried to smile but couldn't. She put the cup down, took out a tissue and dabbed her eyes. I didn't know if there were tears there, or if she was just drying condensed steam that had settled, but she sniffed too, and put her hand out to me. She held mine across the table, clenched it and said, 'Am I making a mistake?'

'What do you mean?'

'With Clive.'

'How do I know? I haven't met the man, so I can't say a thing. I've got to . . .'

'And Canada,' she interrupted. 'What about that?'

'I thought you were all set.'

'I was. I knew exactly what I was going to do, but that was before I saw you again.'

'Oh.'

'I thought I'd be able to cope.'

'Haven't you changed your mind?'

'No.'

'Might you?'

She picked up her tea again and looked out of the window for a minute. Some fishermen walked by in a row, carrying a sausaged net, and an old woman told her dog off for pulling on its lead. A thin layer of cloud obscured the sun so the light was milky and cast no shadows. In the distance, a tanker was heading towards open sea, a pencilly wisp of smoke trailing behind it. The sound of someone peeling potatoes came from the kitchen; sitting in that café was like living in a forgotten black and white movie, where roads are deserted and condiment sets are made out of Bakelite. My mother said, 'I don't know.'

'What don't you know?'

'I was thinking,' she said, and she took a dainty sip of tea, 'how would you like to live in Canada? Clive's got a house in Toronto. It's a lovely place. Clean and fresh, right beside the lake; it would be like starting again for us . . .'

'For you,' I said. 'I don't need to start again.'

'So you don't want to go . . .'

'No.'

'Why not?'

'It's cold, and there's no surf,' I said. 'And the trees are boring.'

'Those are good reasons?'

'No.'

'I'd be there,' she said.

'That's the only reason I would go.'

'So?'

'I've got a place at Exeter.'

'There're universities in Canada.'

'It's not as simple as that . . .'

'No,' she said, 'it's not, is it?' and she turned away. 'I didn't think it would be.'

We sat in silence for two minutes before I said, 'Would you come and live in Exeter?'

She looked back at me. 'I promised him. And I thought . . .' There was another tissue out, and she clenched it to her nose. She gave a little watery blow.

'You thought?'

'I thought this would be so easy. I thought I could do it.'

'Do what?'

'I said goodbye to you before without saying goodbye; maybe I should never have thought I could do it properly.'

I reached out and took her hand. 'Whatever happens, it's not goodbye, not really. You said that.'

'I know.'

'So?'

'So . . .' Suddenly she straightened her back, put her head back, quickly wiped her nose and tucked the tissue up her sleeve. 'So he's coming this afternoon,' she said. 'I love him, Duncan, you understand that?'

'Of course.'

'And I love you.'

I nodded.

'You're part of another love I feel, but grief too. I look at you, and I see your father.'

'Do you?'

She drained. 'Yes.'

I turned to watch some board-sailors walk past the window. Then an old couple strolled past, arm in arm. Then a collarless dog. A seagull flew by and six men fished from the harbour wall. Mother smiled at me as we held hands. 'Yes,' she said again, and we squeezed.

SEVEN

From St Ives we took the coast road, through Zennor and St Just, to Sennen Cove. We didn't talk. We enjoyed each other's company and the scenery.

This part of Cornwall is called West Penwith, and is as wild as any place in the country, with isolated farmhouses in hidden valleys, fields of rocks, ruined engine-houses above abandoned mine-shafts, and smugglers' paths that run through overgrown woods to forgotten coves that have no name, even on the most detailed maps. Streams burble down to the sea, whispering to their banks as they pass. Buzzards hang on thermals, small and hairy old men stand at their doors to watch you pass, women haul bags of stones from their gardens and dump them in meaningless piles. The children here are thin and pale, and hold ages in their eyes. There's an old and dangerous touch in the air you don't find in many other English places; the promise of wicca, triple-headed cats and fire. The sky feels lost, you know you're a stranger. You expect to be watched, and you are. Sweats break out for no reason at all, and every cloud is more than a cloud, it's a threat.

We had to stop for some sheep on the road. They wandered all over the place, oblivious to us. They nibbled at a hedge, then crossed and gathered around a lush patch of grass. One bumped the side of the car, looked up at me and ran off. As we sat and watched, I was slowly overtaken by the strangest, creeping feeling.

It was still out, the windows were wound down, but I felt a

breeze pass my cheek, and I felt it settle behind me, on the back seat. Then there was the faintest smell of raw meat, the flat, fatty smell Dad used to bring home with him, the one that clung to his clothes, his hair and any chair he sat in. It was not overpowering but it was persuasive, always reminding and never letting go, climbing into the nostrils, setting out a camp-bed and lying down for a snooze. It was there then, whispering in the car, twisting around me like smoke. I leant forward and took a deep breath; the sheep bleated, and from a distance, from a very long way away, I heard a single note.

Dad used to whistle as he walked in the back door from work, and Mother would always gently turn him around, point him towards the scullery and say, 'Wash up before you sit down.' She did this every day, but he never told her that she was repeating herself. He had a quiet, perfectly pitched whistle, it was never irritating. He was not one of those people who whistles and forgets he's doing it; he never whistled snatches of a song. He always started at the beginning and went through to the end. He always knew what it was called and who had written it. His volume would increase as he washed, the tunes ringing out over the sound of the running water, echoing off the white tile surround. Now, in the car, with Mother sitting next to me staring absently out of the window at the sheep, this strangest feeling tapped me on the shoulder. When I say it tapped, I don't mean metaphorically; I actually felt a finger's touch, and I swivelled around to look. As I did, my left cheek passed through a cold slice of air that hung in the car like a child's mobile, turning slowly in a draught. 'What?' I said, and Mother said, 'I didn't say anything.'

'No,' I said, 'I felt something.'

'What are you talking about?'

'Someone tapped me on the shoulder.'

My mother looked at me and shook her head. 'Don't be silly,' she said.

'No,' I said, 'I'm not. Really. I felt it . . .' and then, as the sheep took up fresh positions in the road, and Mother began to tap the dashboard with her fingernails – rat-a-tat, rat-a-tat – I heard it. I am not kidding, I couldn't lie; 'Bess, you is my woman now' came in the air, exactly as smoke does, but in sound. It uncurled and twirled and it rubbed against the roof of the car. I cocked my head, I put my fingers in my ears and swallowed deeply. It was not inside my head, it was there. I said, 'Can you hear that?'

'What?'

'Whistling.'

'Whistling?'

'Yeah,' I said.

'Where?'

'Here. In the car.' I narrowed my eyes. 'Listen.'

She cocked her head to listen, and I heard the whole of the first verse . . .

Bess, you is my woman now, you is, you is!
An' you mus' laugh an' sing an' dance for two instead of one.
Want no wrinkle on yo' brow, no how.
Because de sorrow of de past is all done done.
Oh, Bess, my Bess.
De real happiness is jes' begun.

. . . and then there was a pause. The wet, oily smell of the sheep invaded the car, and began to two-step with the whistling, sweeping across a wide marble floor. I thought hard about speaking, but I couldn't help myself. I cleared my throat quietly, and said, 'It's Dad. It's his whistle.'

'Duncan,' said my mother, 'don't be so stupid.'

'I'm not being stupid. Can't you hear it?'

She raised her voice. 'No I cannot,' she said, 'and if this is your way of upsetting me, you're going the right way about it. Your father's dead, so he's not likely to be whistling now, is he? I think your imagination's getting the better of you, so the sooner you get it under control, the better.'

'But I heard him . . .'

'Duncan!' she shouted. Her eyes were wide open and her face was purple; if she could have steamed from her ears, she would have then, there in the car. She bared her teeth and started to shake her head. 'Don't!' she yelled. 'Just don't!'

When was the last time I heard her shout? I had to dredge my mind for the memory; it was definitely in Margate, and I think it was when I dropped her favourite teapot on the floor. It shattered, the pieces flying in every direction; weeks later she was still finding shards of it in unlikely places, and every shard she found would rekindle her anger. It was a blue and white teapot, with tiny little flowers on stalks. When I think about it now, I suppose it was a harbinger; love for a special teapot was a touch of the love for a husband, and every shard was a memory of some pleasant time spent. Or maybe not. I do know that I hate her shout. It's a witch's noise; her neck tightened as the sound shot out, and all the veins stuck out. One sheep looked at the car, there was sheep surprise in its eyes, and then the whistling came back. This time I didn't say anything; I just sat with my eyes closed and listened.

You know the one, the big one. 'Bess, you is my woman now'. Willard White and Cynthia Haymon made the song their own, and Jack Gibbons recorded it as a solo piano piece. When Jack plays, he sounds as though he's got six hands; when my Dad whistled, he sounded as though he had birds backed up his throat. I swear he was there in the back, leaning forward and looking over our shoulders at the sheep.

I opened my eyes. 'Bess,' I said.

'What are you talking about?' Mother looked at me as if I was mad. She looked mad, and I knew I was the only one.

'Nothing,' I said.

She held my eyes in her face for a moment, the whistling continued, and then the sheep parted. I said, 'It doesn't matter,' and we drove on. Dad had his face so close to me that I could feel his breath on my cheek. The tune went right through me and peeled pieces off the top of my head. When I looked at my mother, she was concentrating on the road and her eyes were big and clear, as if she was working something out. She did not know that we had company, or that someone could read her thoughts. I've always thought that at the moment of death you discover all the secrets of the world, and they mean nothing to you because you know them. A mathematical sum is a mystery and a secret until you know the answer, and then it's nothing. A wave is a mystery until you ride it, and though you can learn something about it, it remains. It remains what? I don't know.

Sennen was quiet. A few people were strolling along the beach, and there were two old ladies in the café drinking tea and eating scones, but otherwise we had the place to ourselves. Mother parked, and we walked along the front and down on to the sand. She took my arm and said, 'If I wasn't thinking about going away with Clive, if I hadn't met him, I'd come to Exeter with you tomorrow.'

'But if you hadn't met him, you wouldn't be here now.'

'Maybe not.'

'I'd be putting flowers on your grave.'

'Probably.'

'And anyway, I thought you'd made up your mind. I thought you'd done all the thinking you needed.'

'You've never done that. I knew you were just around the corner, but I never imagined this . . .'

'What?'

She shook her head.

'Second thoughts?' I said.

'Maybe,' she said. 'He's a lovely man. Kind, gentle; everything Dad was. You don't mind me saying that, do you?'

'No.'

'He's all I needed, but then, when I think of Canada . . . it's a long way . . .'

'Maybe . . .' I said.

As we walked, we were pushed by the wind. The tide was out, the waves were weak and broken; they started too late and died too soon, and never rose higher than a foot. 'You know we've been here before?' I said. 'Do you remember?'

'How could I forget?' We walked towards the back of the beach, where there was some shelter, and sat down on a grassy mound. 'Never, ever think I forgot any of the old days.' She suddenly looked fierce. 'If I hadn't had them, I think I would have been alright, but to have them and then have them taken away so quickly, without warning, in a moment; that's the worst thing that can happen. I saw him off to work, and the next man I saw was the policeman telling me he was dead.' She shivered.

I shivered. 'It'll be alright,' I said, but she didn't say anything else.

We had lunch in the café, and it was OK for twenty minutes, until a family came in. We'd been talking about Geography, Marcus and Susan, girlfriends I'd had and marmalade, when the family came in and sat down by the window. There was the husband, the wife, a little boy and a baby in a push-chair. The baby was picked up and sat on the mother's knee, a bottle produced and offered. The little boy started to draw pictures in the condensation that ran down the window, while the father studied the menu. When the baby was settled with its bottle, the mother sat back, sighed deeply and slipped her coat off her shoulders. She was wearing a blue cardigan with a spray of birds down its right side, and her hair was tied in a pony-tail. She put out her hand and gently rubbed her husband's fingers. He looked up from the menu, smiled at her and said, 'What'd you like?'

'You, darling,' she whispered.

He slipped his hand out from underneath hers, reached up and cupped her cheek in his hand. He smiled smiles that could have broken a dog's heart. 'To eat?' he said.

'Still you,' she said.

'Nice,' he said, and they exchanged winks, 'but here and now. On your plate, with a knife and fork . . .'

'What is there?'

'Whatever you want.'

'Prawn sandwiches?'

He looked down the menu. 'OK,' he said, then he turned to the little boy. 'Ben,' he said, 'what would you like to eat?'

'Chips.'

'Chips what?'

'Chips, please.'

'And do you want anything with them?'

'Fingers,' said the boy.

'Fish fingers?'

'Yes.'

'Orange squash?'

'Yes, please.'

The waitress went to the table and took the family's order; she was a small woman and wore a white cap on her head. When she'd left them, the man reached across the table and tweeked the baby's nose. The woman had curly brown hair and a mouth shaped like the roofs that you see on old houses in Holland. She looked down at the baby, then at her husband, who smiled and winked at her. I turned to look at my mother, and tears were streaming down her cheeks.

'Mother,' I said. I scraped my chair towards her, and put

my hand through the crook of her arm. She was holding a tissue to her nose; she blew quietly into it, then searched for another. I gave her my handkerchief. 'What's the matter?'

She heaved.

The family didn't notice us. They were completely absorbed.

'Please. Don't cry.'

'Ssh,' she said, to herself.

'I'm here,' I said.

She blew again, then said, 'I was so sure, so completely sure. I was before you came, and last night, when I went to bed. And when I woke up this morning; but then when we were in St Ives, I couldn't stop thinking. It was when we parked, after what you said, and you were going to the ticket machine in the car park, and I saw you from behind. The shape of your head, your walk, the way your arms hang down. The way you carry your hands with the palms facing outwards . . .'

'I what?'

'Your father used to. I thought I was seeing a ghost . . .'

'A whistle?' I said. She didn't hear me.

'. . . You could be him, twenty-five years ago,' she said. 'He's even in your voice . . .'

'I didn't know.'

'Nor did I.'

She blew lightly again, and said, 'Clive can be like him, but he's different. Does that make sense?'

'Maybe.'

'I was so sure. I am so sure . . .' Her eyes widened, madly, though she was still crying. 'Absolutely. A new life. Begin again, all that.' She nodded towards the family. 'And when they came in . . .'

'What?'

'Didn't you see them?'

'Yes.'

'But you don't remember. No . . .'

'Remember what?'

'When we were here, this same café, the same weather.' She pointed at the little boy. 'You were about the same age, maybe a bit older. And she's got the baby I should have had.'

'Don't,' I said.

'Let me.'

'But don't hurt yourself.'

'No,' she said, but she did not sound convinced, or convincing. 'I'm just afraid.'

'What of?'

'When I see him later, will I be as sure as I should be?'

'Should be?'

'Could be. As I must be.'

I shrugged. 'You know what I'd like, but I wouldn't like it if you did what I want and were unhappy.'

'What?'

'I'm sorry,' I said, 'I don't know.'

She sniffed loudly, wiped her eyes and sat up straight. Now I wanted to cry, and I felt exhausted. My heart swelled in my chest, and then it shrank; I felt it was the size of a town, and then the size of a raisin. It had an awful, ominous stab, a warning and a huge voice. The voice stood in a gale on a high and dangerous cliff, it boomed and echoed, and when I tried to silence it, it blew back at me.

'No,' she said, 'I'm sorry.'

'Don't,' I said.

'Don't what?'

The voice did not stop. 'Nothing,' I said.

'Duncan?' she said, and the word killed me.

'Please . . .'

'Please what?'

I couldn't say. I shook my head. 'Nothing . . .'

She looked at me, held my eyes and then looked away. I looked at her hands, the veins on their backs, her spiny fingers and all the lines that covered her knuckles. Her own hands. They were frozen, and they froze me. 'Duncan, darling?'

'It's alright,' I said.

'But it's not,' she said.

'Mother . . .'

Nothing.

The family's food arrived, and they ate slowly, watching the beach through the picture the little boy had drawn in the condensation. The sea rolled smoothly to the shore, and gulls cruised above it. A fishing boat crossed the horizon, its hull flashing red and white in the sunshine. Mother and I watched it, then looked at each other and then the family; I didn't let go of her, she gripped my hand between her arm and her side. I could feel her ribs and I could feel her breathing; we sat for about twenty minutes, and then drove back to the River Cove Hotel.

EIGHT

Estelle caught me in the corridor outside my room, tapped the floor with her right foot and said, 'What about that drink?' She was wearing a white jumper and baggy blue shorts. Her knees were like pink fruits, and her forehead and cheeks shone. She leant against the door, ran her finger down the bridge of her nose, across her lips and looked straight into my eyes. I got these heavy breaths going off in me, twirly stuff buzzing in my ears, and faint singing in my heels.

'Yeah . . .' I said.

'Have you been crying?'

'No. I got sand in my eyes.' I rubbed them.

'Is that an occupational hazard?'

'Yeah, but I was just talking this morning. The surf wasn't worth it.'

'Does that mean you'll drink twice as much?'

'Might do.'

'Ha!'

'When're you off?' I said.

'Meet you half-nine?'

'Where?'

'Your room?'

'What about your parents?'

'What about them?' She shrugged, and dropped the corners of her mouth. 'Worry you or something, do they?'

'No.'

She had a good look at her fingernails, then back at me. 'Sure about that?' she said. Her eyes were smiling, and some of her hair had slipped out of the white band she wore around her head and was hanging down, brushing her cheek. She had a tiny mole on her neck, beneath her left ear.

'Won't they mind you coming to my room?' I felt my voice about to crack, but I pulled it up in time, slapped it a couple of times, told it to behave and continued with: 'I didn't think staff were meant to fraternise on the premises.'

'Yes.'

'Yes what?'

'Yes they would mind, but who said anything about fraternising? I thought we were going to have a drink. No law against a couple of people having a drink, is there?'

'No.'

'Good.'

'So . . .' I said.

'But if you don't want to risk it, or if you didn't mean what you said, or you're too tired, fair enough. I wouldn't want to make it difficult for you.'

'You won't,' I said.

'Sure about that?'

'Yeah.'

'Good. Then it's half-nine.'

'Yeah.'

She narrowed her eyes at me, flicked at her hair and shuffled her feet. Her shoes sounded like glass skimming across ice. 'Don't be late . . .'

'I won't be.'

I had no idea what to expect. My mother had said Clive was big in every way, but I hadn't guessed how big. He was huge, the most enormous man I had ever seen, but not fat. He was about fifty, his chest was the width of a table, and his thighs were the size of dogs. His arms were long and thick, and his hands were the size of soup plates, with long, slender fingers.

When we shook hands, mine disappeared into his, his fingers were right around it, I looked down and it seemed as though my hand ended in a stump and I was touching his clenched fist with it. I looked up at him and said, 'Hello.'

'Duncan,' he said, in a voice that boomed around the reception. A few guests, sitting in armchairs with newspapers on their laps, stirred in their sleep. 'Diana's told me so much about you,' he said in a lowered voice. 'I've been looking forward to meeting you.'

'Yeah,' I said, and I got my hand back.

His body was enormous, his voice was loud, he was wearing a brown tweed three-piece suit that hung from him like a sack, and massive brown walking shoes, but his head was the most amazing thing about him. It was like the head of a Roman in a museum. It was about a third bigger than a head should be, and his eyes appeared to have hollows at their centres, exactly like you see on ancient sculptures. He had a hedge of grey hair, eyebrows like spindrift, and grooves in both his cheeks that ran in parallel and converging lines to his neck. His forehead was flat and swept with four lines that looked exactly like the outlines of a child's drawing of seagulls.

'Have you had tea?' he boomed.

Mother, who had been standing to one side, watching us, took a step forward and said, 'Not yet.'

Clive looked down at her, and there was love in his eyes, and concern. He touched her gently on the arm, as an area of high pressure will gently prod the low, and the seas will rise to the weather, and he said, 'Let's go and sit down.'

'Lovely,' she said.

'By the window?' he said. 'A view of the sea?'

'Fine.'

I led the way.

We sat in a corner, away from the window. Anything my mother wanted to say to him was kept under the table, and things he had planned to talk about remained with their hands tied and their mouths taped, but he was good at keeping tension away, at keeping the talk going in a friendly, unthreatening way. When he looked at me, he didn't show any nerves, or avert his eyes. He behaved as an uncle you hadn't seen for years would behave, encouraging me to tell him my plans for university, and then about surfing. Mother watched me, she nodded, she shifted in her chair, stiffly. I could see her weighing up, her eyes swivelling from him to me and back again. They hid their thoughts well, she listened to me and nodded at the end of each sentence, as if she hadn't heard what I'd said before. About surfing, he said, 'I've never done it; but I'd like to have a go one day.' He smiled at me and then at Mother, then back at me. 'Do you think I'm too old to start?'

'You're never too old . . .'

'Is it difficult to learn?'

'If you can stand up straight you can surf,' I said.

'Well,' he said, 'I can manage that, but I think I'd need a reinforced board, don't you? I wouldn't want to get out there and have one break in two. That would be most embarrassing, wouldn't it? If I can break a bicycle, I think maybe I'd have a bit of trouble with a surfboard.'

Mother laughed.

'You remember that?' he said, and he laughed with her. The tea cups shook.

'How could I forget?' she said.

Clive leaned forward in his chair and said to me, 'Did she tell you about the bike?'

'No.'

He laughed again. 'We hired some in Norfolk, and they were fine for a few miles, weren't they?'

Mother nodded.

'But then we were riding through this little village, and I

heard something go underneath the saddle. It went "ping" and I felt myself sink a little bit.' He leant forward and touched Mother on the arm again. 'You were in front, weren't you?'

'Yes.'

'I didn't say anything. I thought a spring had worked loose or something, you know, a nut. Nothing important, so I carried on riding, pedalling away, working up a good old sweat. I was looking at the view, the weather was hot. It was a marvellous day, wasn't it?'

'Yes.'

'And then . . .' Clive stopped for a moment, smiling, holding back a laugh. This burst out of his mouth suddenly, he grabbed it and put it back in. ' . . .Then I looked down and noticed that the cross-bar wasn't straight, and then the saddle gave six inches, my knees came up, the chain snapped and I fell off.' Now he laughed properly, and once he started, he couldn't stop. His body heaved at the memory, tears streamed down his cheeks, his chair squeaked and complained. A couple by the window looked towards us, then at each other, and said things under their breath. Mother was laughing too, and I joined in though my heart wasn't in it. I hadn't been there, I don't like cycling, I don't like Norfolk. I was being polite, I wanted a drink, I wanted to leave. I felt like a spare prick at a wedding, it was hard to switch from the mood of the morning to the one Clive brought to the afternoon. We were all making an effort, but the effort was too much. I looked at my watch and then told them I had to make a phone call, but this was a lie.

I lay on my bed. I don't remember what I thought. I had a bottle of wine. I opened it, drank a glass quickly, then poured another, and closed my eyes.

I wasn't going to go to sleep but it came anyway, creeping

up on me like a little bad wave. It folded over me, and I went down. Down, down, down; I met my Dad in a field of ripe corn, and he gave me a look I had never seen before. He was angry with me; I was wearing roller skates, but had not made any tracks as I crossed the field. When he opened his mouth his voice was huge and scared me. 'What's your problem?' he said. He had no fingers at his funeral, he had no fingers in the dream, he pointed to me with his nose, which was enormous. Everything was big. Knock.

I didn't know what my problem was. I pointed to my roller-skates and said, 'Rubber wheels. They make no sound at all.' I pointed behind me, across the acres of susurrating corn.

'And how's your mother?'

'I'm afraid for her.'

'Why?' He whistled at me.

'Because of her hands.'

'Her hands?'

'Her own hands, Dad.'

In my dream, I tasted the wine I'd drunk. Its taste had stayed in my mouth, had lodged behind my teeth and under my tongue. I heard a door knob turn and rattle and another voice, calling my name.

High, flying clouds cast long shadows across the corn; these raced towards my father and me. He said, 'What do you want?'

'You,' I said.

'Impossible,' he said.

'Mother,' I said.

'You've got her.'

'But for how much longer?'

There was no answer.

'How much longer, Dad?'

'That's not for me to say.'

'Who can?'

'She can.'

'She wouldn't tell me,' I said.

'Have you asked her?'

'How can I?'

'Have you tried?' he said.

'No'

'Why not?'

'How can you ask someone if they're going to?'

'Going to what, Duncan?'

'You know . . .'

'No I don't.'

'You're dead. You know everything.'

'What makes you think that?'

'It's a feeling I've always had.'

He laughed.

'What's funny?' I said.

'Nothing.' His voice hardened, and violins started to play. It was Gershwin again, 'Bess' again. 'There's nothing funny about using your own hands on yourself.'

'So you do know!'

'It's what you were thinking.'

'How do you know?'

'I know everything . . .'

'There!' I said, and the violins were joined by cellos, and then Willard and Cynthia. 'That's what I thought.'

'But is what you think worth thinking?'

The music got louder, and I heard a knock on a door. 'I don't know. What do you think?'

Another voice called 'Duncan?'

'Who's that?' said Dad.

'Who's what?'

Double-bass, and now woodwind and brass. The voices caressed each other, like they were made of skin. 'There's someone calling.'

'Duncan!'
'I don't know,' I said.
'You'd better answer the door.'
'Why?'
'Answer it!'
Pop.
'Duncan!'
I woke with a start. It was dark. I turned on the light and blinked. My hair was sticking up, and I felt as though the sandpaper men had set up home in my mouth. I heard a single note, and then it popped like a bubble in front of me. I got out of bed and opened the door. My mother was standing there. 'Are you alright?' she said.
'Yeah.' I let her in. She was alone. 'What about you?'
'Hungry. We're going to have some supper.'
'What time is it?'
'Eight.'
'Eight? God.' I went to the sink and washed my face. 'I fell asleep.'
'I was knocking for ages.'
'Sorry.'
'Do you want to join us?'
'I don't know . . .'
'Please.'
'Mother . . .'
'Don't you like him?'
'Yeah, he's great.' I dried my face. 'Really. It was just a bit of a shock.'
'What sort of shock?'
'He's not what I expected.'
'What did you expect?'
'Someone, I don't know, someone more like Dad.'
'He's more like Dad than you think.'
'Is he?'

'Yes. And he likes you too.'

'He doesn't know me.'

'No,' said my mother, 'but he doesn't need to. He's very intuitive.'

'Good for him.'

My mother took my hand and said, 'This is more difficult for me than I ever imagined and, believe me, it's more difficult for him than you'd think. All that cheery chappy stuff; he's very good at putting it on. All he really wants to do is be friends with you.'

'I know that.'

'Are you going to take him surfing?'

I laughed now. 'I don't know.'

'It would be the best thing you could do. He's keen. He'll do anything once.'

'I'll think about it.'

'It would make me happy too. If that's any help to you.'

'Mother,' I said, 'if it'll make you happy . . .'

She let go of my hand. 'Thank you, dear.'

'But I don't think I'll come down to eat. I'll have a sandwich up here.'

She nodded, she did not try to persuade me otherwise. 'Is that going to be enough for you?'

'Yes.'

She looked at me, longingly, confused and thin. 'It's going to be alright, isn't it?'

'I hope so.'

'Say you know so.'

'I can't.'

'I know, but . . .'

'Do you think it's going to work out?' I raised my voice. 'Really? If one of us has to go, how can it?'

'Don't talk like that.'

'I don't want to pretend.'

'Do you think I do?'

'I wonder.'

Now she raised her voice. 'I know what I've got to do, Duncan. Don't think I haven't spent the last six months dreading today. I might look calm enough, but I'm not, I'm all over the place.'

'And Clive? Is he all over the place?'

'Didn't you hear what I said? You . . . you must be pulling him apart. He always wanted children, but he never had the chance. You're probably the closest he'll ever come to one.'

'Is that meant to make me feel wanted?'

'You're wanted whatever happens,' she said.

'Am I?'

My mother didn't answer. She looked at me, then turned and walked to the door. She pointed to the bottle on my table and said, 'Don't drink too much.'

I had my eyebrows up at her.

'See you in the morning.'

'I'll be here,' I said.

I never needed fucking more, to have it done to me, and to do it. I never had the feeling growing so badly in me, the desperate swell, the swimming fingers and slight headache. The jagged lines of light when I closed my eyes, the dry mouth and uncontrollably lively right leg; I had a tepid bath but that didn't help. I had some sandwiches; they were tasty but didn't help. I lay back on the bed and read a magazine, I sat in a chair and watched television, I stood at the window and watched the sun sink behind the black cliffs and deserted path; nothing did it for me. I listened to the burble of diners beneath me, the clatter of knives and forks, and the faint creaks that crept through the hotel. I played with some loose skin on my big toe, and fiddled with some nasal hair. I waited.

Waiting slows time, and gives tiny things importance. For

five minutes I stared at the handle on the drawer of my bedside cabinet. It was made of brass, curly and shining. It was stiff, so that instead of hanging down limply as it should have, it stuck out at an angle, as if it was being held up by an invisible hand. There was a blemish on it, a dark stain, like a mole. When I think of hands, I think of Dad's accident. A bizarre and gruesome accident, and it needn't have happened. Dad's devotion to his work-force, his desire to check that the workers who operated the mincers were happy, and that the mincers weren't jamming again. My bedside cabinet was made of polished pine, like the big bed I lay on. I had a patterned blue and white duvet, and fat pillows. The television was on with the volume down, the sound of the sea drifted and drifted and drifted, all in time with my heart.

The loose skin on my toe was very irritating. There's meat for you. You can forget in sex, and though it's no joke, the forgetting part is serious. You can lose yourself in another person, get inside them and disappear, remove your mind and balance it over a fire; that's sex. I was working up to Estelle. She knocked on the door and I got up to answer it.

She was wearing a green T-shirt and a short white skirt. Her hair was down, she was carrying a bottle of wine. When I opened the door she slipped quickly inside, went to the window and closed the curtains. OK,' she said. 'Safe!'

'Where are you?' I said.

'Here!'

'No. Where did you say you were?'

'Having a bath, then I told them I was getting an early night.'

'Won't they look in on you?'

'Hey!' she said. 'Don't worry.' She put the bottle on the table, and took out a corkscrew. I fetched another glass from the bathroom. She pulled the cork quickly and expertly, and poured. 'Mind if I put my feet up?

Be my guest.'

'No,' she said, 'you're our guest,' and she kicked her shoes off and lay on the bed. She drank half a glass, sighed, said, 'Ah. That's better,' and closed her eyes. I turned the television off, and lay down next to her.

'Hard day?' I said.

'Yeah.'

'Your old man's a slave-driver.'

'He's a prick.'

'I'm sorry.'

'Don't be,' she said, 'he can't help it; I think he was born that way.'

'No,' I said, 'I'm sorry for you . . .'

'Are you?'

'I certainly am.'

'Well, thanks,' she said, and drank some more.

I watched her breasts as she breathed. They rose, and then they fell. They rose again, then down again. They were up, they were down. When they were up, her nipples showed, when they were down, her nipples flattened. Then, after about a minute, her nipples were up when the breasts were down as well as up, and she tightened her arms. Her hands lay on her stomach, holding her glass. Her legs were apart, the left bent at the knee, the right tucked underneath it. She finished the drink. 'More?' I said.

'Yeah.'

'There you go.'

'So how's it been with your mother?'

'Weird,' I said. 'I don't know. I'm thinking one thing one minute, and another the next, and all the time I'm worried. Scared.'

'Why?'

'Because . . .' I looked at my fingernails, and white spots that were creeping up them.

'Yeah?'

'A couple of years ago, she tried to top herself, and I think she's still got it in her. That look in her eyes, you know?'

'Yeah.'

'You do?'

'You can't miss it. It's like being watched by a ghost.'

'Exactly,' I said. 'It's deadly, but I don't know; maybe she'll be OK. I met her bloke today, and I suppose he's exactly the sort she needs.'

'Dr Noberts?'

'Yeah, Noberts!' I cried, and I kicked my legs in the air. 'What a name!'

'It's brilliant!'

'He's alright.'

'Have you seen his head?'

I looked at her. 'Of course I've seen his head! How could you miss it?'

She laughed, grabbed my arm and held me tight. 'And it was alright?'

'I suppose so. I haven't seen Mother for eight years, I want to get to know her again, but then I've got him too, and he's pulling her one way, and I'm pulling the other. I'm jealous, but I suppose he's thinking the same. I want her to be happy, but I want more of her than I'm going to get.'

'What do you mean?'

'They're going to Canada.'

'Nice place.'

'Yeah,' I said.

'When?'

'Monday.'

'Oh.'

'I told her she could come and live with me. I could see she was thinking about it, it confused her. She's very proper, very correct, she won't show what she really feels, so it gets bottled up, and then it blows out the top of her head. I don't want to give her too much to think about, but I can't help it. And it's all so quick, such bad timing. Why couldn't she have organised it so I saw her one day, him a month later, news of Canada the month after that?'

'She wants to get it over quick,' she said.

'I'm not something she's got to get over!'

'She knows that. But the telling you, all that. She knows what she wants, she wouldn't want to be sitting on her arse for months, waiting for the right moment.' She tipped her head back and scratched her neck. 'Do it all at once; it's what I'd do.'

'Would you?'

'Yeah.'

I had a good look at her face. She opened her mouth to ask another question, but I put my fingers to my lips and then to hers. She let out a little puff of air as I touched her, then rolled her head back and narrowed her eyes.

I kissed her neck; as I touched it, it stretched, her skin smelt of an airing cupboard. It was soft and warm, I paddled my right hand over the duvet to her stomach, took her glass, put it on the bedside cabinet, and paddled back.

She unbuttoned my shirt and began to rub my chest, I worked slowly over her stomach, and it rippled beneath her T-shirt, exactly right. I pulled the T-shirt up and it was perfect, a pool of skin, flattened at either side where it spread over her waist, wobbling slightly. I kneaded it with my fingers into little humps and bumps, dropped my head and sucked some of it into my mouth. She whined, she took one of my legs and gripped it between her thighs, and started up a gentle rocking motion. The bed began to whine, I kicked out with my free leg and pushed a blanket on to the floor.

I had the sound of waves, I took the T-shirt in both hands

and eased it up, keeping it tight across her breasts, which went up and down all the time, three inches beneath me; she was lying flat now, and I was supporting myself on my elbow, and here's the good bit, I lifted her T-shirt up and pulled it over her head. Ever seen God? I did. They were incredible. She was incredible. She sat up, lifted her arse, pulled her skirt off, tossed it across the room and lay back again. I had my trousers off, she was like cake, a well-cooked omelette, the speed and shape of Supertubes, the smell of the fish factory a mile up the road from Supertubes, the colour of a hazel nut, anything off The Waterboys' second album, a crucial configuration of pressure systems over the North Atlantic, Portuguese wine, Irish airs, English marmalade; I lowered myself, and began to lick her nipples.

Her nipples were hard, sticking up as if they were trying to listen to me. I cupped both her breasts and put my face into them. You duck-dive a tall breaking wave; anticipate where the lip will fall, push your weight forward, submerge the board and take a deep breath. Go down with the board, close your eyes, underneath and out the other side. She grabbed my waist and pulled me on to her, pulled my head up and kissed me on the mouth. 'Yes,' she whispered. I thought 'Yes?' She put her tongue in my mouth and began to polish the inside of my cheeks. I fought back with my tongue, she drew her fingernails lightly down my back, on to my buttocks, around them and back again. We allowed the tips of our tongues to fight, and I moved down to have another go at her breasts, this time their sides.

Sometimes, Susan makes a sweet Mexican jelly out of milk and caramel that sits on the dish exactly like the flanks of Estelle's breasts sat on her chest. The jelly and the breasts had the same sheen, not shiny but lightly reflective; I blew on Estelle's, licked them and rubbed the spit with my finger. She pushed down, hooked me around the waist with her legs, and turned on to her side. Then she pushed me down, I lay beneath her, she looked down at me.

God, I had a stalk on me you wouldn't believe, like a tennis-racquet handle. I was keeping up these rhythmic thrusts, I could feel sweat chatting on my forehead. It was popping out in spots all over, each spot was jealous of the one next to it, her breasts were hanging down, I reached up and weighed them in my hands, she reached down, wrapped her fingers around my prick and tucked its tip up her. She made a buzzing-bee sound through her teeth, pushed down, slowly, her head back, her back arched, her stomach rippled in tiny waves from the top to the bottom. I reached out and smoothed them as she moved, circled her navel with my finger, she lay down and started to grind seriously, clenching me inside, wet ran out of her, and down my leg.

'Get a life!' she cried.

'Got one already!' I wailed.

'Have some more!'

'Cheers!'

'More?'

'Go!'

Someone banged on the door.

'God!' she whispered.

'What's the matter?'

'My old man. Any money you like.' She jumped off me, slipped off the bed, grabbed her shirt and skirt and skipped towards the bathroom. As she passed the television she turned it on, turned the sound up and put her finger to her lips. As she moved about the room, her flesh rose and fell, her breasts swung from one side to the other, the insides of her thighs glistened. She passed her hand over her pubes, held her palm out to me and disappeared into the bathroom. I pulled on my pants, the knock came again, I narrowed my eyes and unlocked the door.

Estelle's old man whipped his head away from the door and touched his ear.

'Yeah?' I said. 'What's the problem?'

'Have you,' he said, and his voice was mean and pinched, like a waterskier's, 'seen Estelle?'

'Estelle?' Brilliant.

'My daughter. She works behind reception.'

'Oh,' I said, 'yeah. Saw her this afternoon. At tea . . .'

'I'm talking about now,' said the old man, and he jabbed a finger at me.

'What are you getting at?'

'I heard voices,' he whined.

'So? I'm watching telly.' I opened the door a tad, so he could see it flickering in the corner. A woman with big hair was walking across a street with a policeman.

He took a step forward, so his right foot was in the room. 'So you haven't seen her since tea-time?' He sniffed the air. 'What's that smell?'

'What smell?'

He looked at me with a very stupid expression on his face, as if, for a moment, he'd forgotten who he was. I looked back with disgust. He looked with suspicion. I looked with innocence. He looked like he couldn't have been her father. No way. I looked very happy. He sniffed again and said, 'Perfume.'

'Isn't it nice?' I said. 'My mother was here.'

'Your mother,' he said, raising the pitch of his voice, 'is in the dining room. Has been for the last hour and a half.'

'Enjoying her supper, is she?'

'Dinner,' he said, 'dinner.'

'Dinner.'

'Yes,' said the fart, 'I think she is.'

'Look,' I said, and now I lowered my voice, gave it some growl and thinner lips, 'what do you want? I'm allowed to watch telly, aren't I? I didn't see any notice saying it was forbidden. And supper – sorry – dinner, isn't a compulsory meal, is it?'

He put on an apologetic, hurt face, and stepped back into the corridor. 'Of course it's not forbidden,' he said, 'of course not.' He scratched his chin, sniffed again and put his hands together. 'You carry on.' I think he might have been in the army once; I waited for him to salute me, but he didn't. He took another step back. I said 'Goodnight,' and closed the door. I stood still for a minute and listened for his footsteps in the corridor. They didn't start immediately; there was some frustrated shuffling for a moment, then he began to walk slowly away. I turned, looked at the television, and then went to the bathroom.

Estelle was naked, sitting on the side of the bath, biting the side of her right hand; when she took it away, she laughed, threw her head back and said, 'The best yet!'

'Get this a lot, do you?'

'Yeah.'

'And I did alright?'

She reached out, put her arms around my neck and pulled me towards her. 'You were perfect.'

We slipped. It was a mess. She was doubled up in the empty bath, and I was on top of her, bent the other way, my feet pointing at the ceiling and the top of my head banged against the side of the bath. I got my hands out from under her and pushed up. She pulled me down again and said, 'How about it?'

'Any time you like,' I said.

'Sure about that?'

'Yeah.'

'You know what it means?' she said.

'I hope so.'

She laughed, pulled me back to the bedroom, on to the

bed, and lay down with her feet on the floor; I knelt down and nestled my face between her legs. She closed them lightly and rubbed my cheeks with her thighs. Portugal, the road from Lisbon to Peniche, the first sight of Supertubes. A perfect offshore wind, left-handers at low tide, right-handers at high, not too hairy, but hairy enough. On the lip it was tight, and off it I was in this long, tight barrel, running low and hard towards the shore. The roar was steady and heavy, there was light foam flying off the lip, the sun was low in the evening, I was alone. As I picked up speed, Estelle took her breasts in her hands and squeezed them together, it was like fucking in a fruit market, there was an angel for every day of the week, and two on Saturday. She wailed and moaned and I grunted, then made heavy blowing noises, she pushed towards me and pushed her nipples into my eyes. Death by sex, love by sex, sex loves woman, she put her legs in the air, clamped me hard and started up a long, low whine that came from her stomach, hit her throat with a ping and came out like a shrunk song. The bed was squeaking, creaking and bending, the sound of the sea bashing the rocks was in the air. Estelle gripped my buttocks, and began to sink her fingernails into them. To begin with, all I felt was a pricking sensation, then this grew to a stabbing, overtaken by a hollow, dull feeling. This was immediately covered by great pain as she dug all her nails, all at once, into me. I yelled, she flipped me over, we were on the floor, her nails did not give up, she smothered my face with her breasts, and gripped hard with her legs, she was rocking backwards and forwards, I could not escape, I did not want to, the barrel was as long as Supertubes in the longest dream I ever had, each yard was tighter than the last but it never became too tight, I never wiped out there. I was confident because she was the wave I had always wanted, she was mine before I saw her, and I belonged to her. I began to disappear into Estelle, she was all over me, all around, her stomach wanted to spread out, curl up around my back; her nipples pierced my eyes and began to weep, her breasts folded my face and tucked gently into themselves.

She released her hold and swivelled over, lying with her stomach on the bed, her knees on the floor and her arse in the air. I pushed off for a forward bottom turn, then pulled back and flipped into a long backhand re-entry. It was perfect, slow and clean, foam was flying off the lip in tiny spits, we began to buck wildly, it began to whisper in my ear, it began to play a tune on my teeth, it began to flash messages in front of my eyes, it began to come, it began to prick the tips of my fingers, it started to pass messages from my knees to my brain that said go limp, it began to bang on my balls and announce it was a through train, please stand back from the edge of the platform and will the busker on platform four desist, and it was a train with curtained windows passing through a German forest, and behind every window a woman was holding on to me, the train whistled, the Portuguese tubes roared towards the shore, it was the middle of the week, there was no one about, and it began to make my hair stand up on end. It was a line of cars waiting at traffic-lights, and when the lights changed, all the cars moved forward at once, banging into each other, up-ending like dominoes and falling down an impossibly small hole in the road. It was a trip on a fast bike down the French coast to Hossegor, where Napoleon diverted a river and created some of the finest surf in Europe. It was taking German Bunkers, La Piste or Le Gravier, waves so terrifying that they boil sweat. It was back to the train in the German forest, and all the women leaving their compartments, carrying glasses of wine in one hand and plates of lobster in the other. Lobsters snapping, birds flying and sheep moving across fields in the night. The smell of sheets and bouillabaisse, gun metal and tea. All my senses screamed mercy, but none of them meant what they said; I knocked them back against the ropes, picked them up, slapped them around and knocked them back again. Sweat was pouring down my back, it was hot in that room. The television showed an advert for coffee. Estelle tipped her head back, looked at me and cried out. 'This,' I said, and came as deep as I could, 'is the sea!'

NINE

In the morning, Estelle was up and behind the reception. As I staggered past her, I said, 'I think I broke it.' She said, 'Want me to mend it?' I said, 'It needs careful handling,' and her father came out of his office. He stood behind her, focused on me, and I listened to his brain clicking. The smell of toast was in the air. I smiled at him, then back at her, and went to have my breakfast.

Clive and Mother were already eating. They were glowing and pink, they beamed at each other, for a second they both looked at me as if I was a stranger, then Clive stood up and Mother reached out and held my hand. For the first time in over eight years, I saw her eyes spark, and her lips were shining. 'Duncan,' she said, sweetly, her voice rising up to touch the ceiling, then floating down to brush my face, 'did you sleep well?'

'Yes thanks.' I sat down and winced. I shifted, winced again, and got as comfortable as I could.

'Are you quite alright?'

'Yeah . . .'

'We were worried about you.'

'Worried?'

'When you didn't come down for dinner. I thought you might be ill, but Clive said you were just tired. That was it, wasn't it?'

'Yeah,' I said.

'You had some sandwiches?' she asked.

'Yeah.'

She touched my face. 'You do look a little drawn. Are you sure you're OK?'

'Yes, Mother. Really.'

Estelle's mother came over and stood by me with a severe look on her face. She had dangerous lines around her mouth and eyes, and a tiny tongue poking out. It disappeared. She held her pad and pencil and snapped, 'Tea, is it?'

'Please.'

'Toast and marmalade?'

'Thank you.'

'Is that a yes?'

'Yes.'

Estelle's mother jotted, slapped the pad into her breast pocket, turned around and stalked off, ignoring a call from another table for more coffee. I looked out of the window.

The sun was weak, a heavy cover of grey cloud hung over the cliffs, and the air was muggy.

'She was a bit off,' said my mother.

I shrugged. 'Nothing to do with me.'

My mother smiled, Clive laughed and looked across the dining room to the door that led to the reception. I leant back and glanced in that direction too; I saw Estelle's sleeve and her hand. She was writing something in the register. The hand disappeared. Mother said, 'What are you doing today?'

'Me?' I said.

'Yes. We thought we'd go for a walk on the cliffs, maybe take picnic. Why don't you come along?'

She was very happy. Clive smiled at her, reached across the table and touched her hand. 'No,' I said, 'you don't want me around. I think I'll go to Sennen, see what's happening.'

'What makes you think we don't want you around?' said Clive. 'Please. Do come.'

'No,' I said, 'really,' as Estelle's mother came back with a pot of tea and banged it down on the table in front of me. She smelt of fried food and mothballs. 'Go on your own . . .'

'Alright,' said Mother, 'but if you change your mind . . .'

'Thanks.'

It was great to be back in the Beetle, alone, the board slicing the air, The Waterboys playing.

Who shot the arrow?
How high did it fly?
When he tipped it
With poison
Did he even know why?
What unseen hand
Brought him
Face to face to face to face with
All this and more
In a pagan place?

There are surfers who only listen to sixties music; The Beach Boys, cruisin' music, but that's lightweight stuff, virgin tunes with no balls. Mike Scott writes what he knows, and he knows about depth. It is definite and sure, rooted in conviction; I could surf with him. I banged the steering-wheel as I drove, and yelled the song at the top of my voice. 'In a Pagan Place!' 'Come into my parlour, Sail in at my shore, Drink my soul dry, There is always more . . .' I put my fingers to my nose and smelled them. I hadn't washed that morning, I wouldn't unless I had to. No smell is like that one, no taste like it. The song finished, I flipped the tape back to the beginning and listened to it again.

I'd watched Mother and Clive leave the hotel and climb the path to the cliffs. They were arm in arm, they were chatting, she pointed to something at sea, he laughed. He was wearing a huge tweed hat with a feather stuck in the band and heavy walking boots. They saw me before they turned the corner at the grassy plateau, and I waved. They waved back, and then disappeared.

I ached, and my aches had aches. My whole body was filled with silver. Estelle was paddling in my blood; I drove with a stupid smile on my face and the sight of her breasts in front of me. Ten-year-old Spanish girls have visions of the Virgin Mary, Scottish soccer players have dreams of winning the World Cup. Coal-miners dream in black, brewers dream in smell-o-vision. I had Estelle's breasts hanging in front of me, her thighs were like a meal. I sang too loud and drove too fast; when I saw the sea between folds in the hills, I looked at it and not the road.

No love no gain, no gain no pain. No pain no loss, no loss no gain, no love. Nothing like a load of nonsense to fill your head when you're in that state. Nothing like a load of nothing to make you know when you meet something. If you find it, enjoy it, but never think you can keep it. You've no right to want to keep anything. I was in a great mood. Surf comes around again, but wearing different clothes. When I got to Sennen, I parked and stared at it for five minutes.

The big waves were three days away; the Sennen breaks were nothing special, but they were swollen with promise. The water had the translucent look it grows before a storm, a threatening green with a hint of blue, broken here and there with ripples of white. I changed, took my board to the beach and stood at the edge.

The line between the sea and the land stretches like a ribbon of heat; I stood on it, and it warmed my feet. I imagine the heat and it's there; I took a step into the water, then a step back on to the sand, then into the water again. There was no one else about, the air was still and thick, the sky had yellow edges. I laid the board down, brushed it and began to wax it.

I used the strawberry Sex Wax that Susan and Marcus had

given me for my birthday. It's the best cool-water wax, the flavour doesn't matter, nor the colour. Don't let it stand on your car dashboard on a hot day or it'll melt and make a terrible mess; store it in a cool place. Apply it to the board with care, gently rubbing on a thin layer. Too thick and it will attract sand and grit. Concentrate, take your time and do yourself a favour.

I fastened my leash and walked into the sea. A dead wave broke over my knees, I scooped up some water and splashed it on my face, licked my lips. I went up to my waist, floated the board beside me, jumped on and began to paddle out.

The sets were nothing. I paddled lazily, three strokes at a time, then a break, then another three. The currents were weak, there were no sea-birds in the sky, I passed a frond of weed, waving like fingers as it floated to the shore. Or Estelle's hair.

That was another thing. I never thought about a woman's hair before. I never wished plump sex would have a particular kind of cut, colour or length. Estelle's hair, when released from the white band she wore for work, was big, brown and light. I could get my fingers into it and rummage around, put my face in and breathe it into my mouth. It filled my mouth, it built me up and capped me off. It built scaffolding around my eyes that shook in windy weather. I have my hair short now, spiky on top, and my chin shaved tight. When Estelle held my head, she held it like a big egg. Careful you don't drop it.

I paddled fifty yards, then relaxed between a long set and watched the sea breaking over the nose of the board. It came in tiny waves that formed and broke in the same way as the big, some breaking quickly, others making barrels that ran to the left and right, down the rails of the board to the fins. I stopped one of these with my finger, and paddled on.

A gull came and swooped me as I caught the first wave, a soft, clean and dainty thing that came slowly, rising in a flat curve that picked me up and curled left. I pushed up and crouched, letting it do the work for me; the gull swooped and cried at me, so close that I could feel the rush of air as it broke over me. I went for a little forehand cutback, I surfed a pair, then laid back and took the rest of the wave to the shore. It broke gently, spilling along its length with a thin and graceful roll. It roared quietly, rustling the sand on the beach like wind on curtains. It was my mother walking across a room, it was the sound of my mother's voice uncoiling in the air. I paddled out again and took another.

This one was dirtier, longer and kinked in the middle, and when it hit the reef, it seemed to run backwards. I tried to surf its length, but it began to break up before I got half-way. I let it swallow me up, and I let the next set break over me. It tried to steal my board, but I didn't give a fuck. I yelled and I swallowed, and I floated. I gave each wave a name I forgot, but it didn't matter, and I didn't care at all.

I surfed quietly all morning. I caught nothing that would interest the rip-and-slash boys, or anyone from Hawaii, but it was bewitching, hushed and warm. The muggy air muted sound, so the noise of the running board, the cries of gulls and the rush of the sea seemed to come from a distance. I was on the longest wave of the morning, cutting into its lip and back again, dipping and crouching to keep the speed, when I saw a car park next to the Beetle, and a woman got out. She shaded her eyes, I looked up and leant forward. Estelle. I fell off and hit my head on the bottom. Wipeout. Deliberate. His own fault.

I hit the bottom face on, mouth open, and filled with sand. I shot up spluttering, released the leash and let the board drift ahead of me. I spat and splashed water into my mouth, and swam after the board. Estelle waved and came running down the beach.

'What's the matter?' she yelled. I hauled myself up the beach. 'Too much for you?'

'It's not much,' I said, and I pointed to the sea, 'but it doesn't matter.' I looked across the bay from one end to the other, up and down and roundabout. 'It's beautiful, isn't it?'

'Certainly is,' she said, and she smacked my arse.

'Ouch!' I yelled.

'My pleasure.'

We went to the café Mother and I had visited the day before. We ordered lemonades, and when the waitress brought them she said, 'Close, isn't it? Doesn't matter if you open the windows, it don't do you no good.' She pointed outside. 'We need a storm. A good gale; that'd clear the air.'

'There's one coming,' I said.

'How do you know?' she said.

'I saw the weather forecast,' I said.

'You don't want to take no notice of weather forecasts; they're nothing but rubbish and lies. They never get it right, and all they do is get more clothes.'

'Sorry?'

'More suits, pullovers, cardigans, you name it.'

'Eh?' I said.

'Weather forecasters,' said the waitress. Estelle held her hand to her mouth and began to rock with silent mirth. 'Every time I see them they're wearing something different.'

'Are they?'

'Yes,' said the waitress. She leaned towards me and said, 'Is your young lady alright?'

'She's fine,' I said.

'Oh, good. I wouldn't like to think it was the cakes, only they've been hanging about a bit.'

Estelle exploded. She laughed like a drain, rocking backwards and forwards in her chair. The waitress stood back, scratched her head and said to me, 'You sure she's alright?'

'Quite sure,' I said.

We didn't have any cake.

Another surfer appeared in the car park, got out and stared at the sea. He had his board strapped to the roof of his car; as he watched the sets, and smelled the air, he rubbed his hand up and down the rail of the board, and his lips moved.

'Your mother,' said Estelle, 'I'd have half a dose of what she was on this morning. She looked a bit happy . . .'

'She is.'

'Everything for breakfast too. Cereal, eggs and bacon, sausage, toast, the lot. Where does she put it all? Watching her's enough to put you on a diet . . .'

'Don't,' I said.

'What?'

'Go on a diet.'

'Why not?'

'I like you as you are.'

'Well,' she said, and she patted her stomach, 'you're too late. I'm on one, not that it makes any difference. I came out fat, I was a fat girl, I'm fat now . . .'

'It's not fat,' I said, 'it's flesh.'

'Ha!' She blew lemonade over me. 'It's fat!'

'Plump . . .'

'Fat, plump, plump, fat. There's size ten and there's fat.'

'That's bollocks.'

'Anywhere you want to look, Dunc. Open your eyes. Mags, telly, ads, holiday brochures. You make an effort, but really, I don't give a toss.' She patted her stomach again. Good to see, that. 'I like me,' she said.

'I like you,' I said.

'Yeah?'

'Yeah.'

'And I like you,' she said. 'Can't be bad, can it?'

'No.'

'Not many to the pound, but what you get's quality.'

'Too true.'

'Unlike you,' she said, and she pinched my waist. It hurt. 'Fancy it tonight?'

'Do I?'

'I do,' she said.

The waitress came back, wiped her hands on her apron and said, 'And another thing.'

'What's that?'

'The one with the glasses. He doesn't spend any money on suits, and it shows, doesn't it? He's so scruffy. I saw him once, and he had a button missing on his cardigan. I ask you; a cardigan! Amount of money you pay for a licence, you'd think they'd sort him out. It's a disgrace,' she said, and she shuffled off again.

TEN

I dozed in the afternoon, on the bed with the windows open. It was sticky. The curtains barely moved, the sea had flattened, the cliffs were spread with a dead, fat heat. Gulls cried but their voices were swallowed by the fug. I lay naked, flat on my stomach with antiseptic cream on my buttocks, and I breathed slowly. I dribbled lightly on the pillow, and my body gave off a sour smell.

The air crept over my body like greased paper, clinging and sticking to every crack and crevice it could find. It spoke to the backs of my knees and sang to my armpits, and when it moved to my ears it traced their outlines with its fingers. When I moved, the sheet gripped me and would not let go; I left damp patches on it, each one in the shape of a different Mediterranean island. Here was Corsica and here was Ibiza, where my cheek had been was Cyprus, and where my toes had fidgeted from one place to the next was the Cyclades. Crete was one foot and Corfu was another. Each smelt of cotton and sweat, fish, soap and butter. These smells reminded me of when I was a child and I used to carry a filthy comfort rag with me. They drifted with my thoughts, flicking at their edges, tickling my nostrils and then creeping into my head. I felt sapped and weak; I was lying flat, though now and again I thought I was sliding down a long, gentle slope through a swamp, past snapping animals that wouldn't snap because of the heat. Very quiet and slow slide guitar music echoed in my head, and the sound of a low singing voice floated in the air. I closed my eyes and concentrated on trying to guess the exact combined weight of Estelle's breasts.

I slept in short bursts, picking up dreams as you would pick up pictures by popping in and out of a row of houses with televisions on. Here's a scene from a film about monkeys, here's a scene from an American soap and there's something about hats and how rhinoceros foreplay lasts a month. Back to the monkeys and then on to a documentary about women in Peru. Then a programme about parents, and how jealous they can be of their children. How they want their children to do well, but they won't encourage them. How some fathers believe that their sons are for ever twelve years old, they will not let them grow up. Now these people believe that sex is dirty. You ask them why, and they put their fingers to their lips and go 'Ssh!' You wonder; how did these people fuck? Did they ever do it in a car, or on a kitchen table, in a garden shrubbery? All the hang-ups one generation passes to another, and how the last two generations have broken the mould. Then, suddenly, back to the monkeys. The monkeys are popular, far more popular than you'd think. They're fucking in the trees. Then a scene from *Endless Summer*, another scene from *Endless Summer*, a Californian wave that breaks as high as the world, rubs the sun and hangs over all the surfers who have ever lived, then back to the monkeys.

Then my eyes were open, my sight was clear, the curtains puffed, the faintest of breezes stabbed the air and pushed through the room. I tilted my head to catch it, and in that atmosphere it was like being touched by a cool hand. The low was filling, the swell was building, the wind was turning to face me. I pulled myself up, lay on my side and drank a glass of water. I got up, put a towel around my waist and stood on the balcony.

The air was still close, as close as it could be without being liquid. When it touched my skin it felt as though it was coating me. I took a deep breath, it was like taking in warm milk. I coughed and my cough melted in front of me, a pair of walkers on the cliff path moved through a dull haze. They were talking to each other; the sound of their voices crept towards me like syrup. I went to the bathroom, had a tepid shower and brushed my teeth.

My mother came to my room. She and Clive had had a wonderful day, she was so happy, and when I saw her that happy, I was happy too. We were both happy, the room was our happy place, and we had a cup of tea to celebrate. The air smelt of roses and cream, and bells sounded in it. 'Whatever you want, Mother, is what I want. It makes me want you more than ever, but I don't want that to make you sad. Let it make you happier. You're getting a life, I'm getting you. It's going to be OK.'

'I'm so pleased,' said Mother. Her eyes were wild with joy, almost dangerous.

'And how's Clive?'

She blushed. When her cheeks pink, she looks ten years younger. The colour runs on to her nose and it begins to glow like a traffic light. 'Wonderful,' she said. 'You wouldn't think a man his size could be so gentle, but he is. Have you seen his fingers?'

'I noticed them.'

'Every time I touch them I think about the lives he's saved with them.' She smiled to herself, for him, then at me. 'He does so much good in the world.'

'I know.'

'And he's so funny. He makes me laugh all the time.'

'Great.'

'You mean that?'

'Mother,' I said, and I hugged her. 'He's all I hoped he'd be. I've seen you together, I'm not stupid.'

She cupped my chin. 'I know that.'

'It's a shame we couldn't have had longer together now; I wish you'd told me where you were earlier, but I know why you wanted to do it like this. All the birds with one stone, that sort of thing.'

'The times I thought . . .'

'No,' I said, 'really. I know.'

'Do you?'

I held the silence for a moment, gave it a book to read, walked it to Thurso and back, gave my mother's eyes the definite fix, and said, 'Yes.'

'And you're coming down to dinner tonight? We're going to have a bottle of champagne.'

'Champagne?'

'Yes.'

'I'll be there,' I said.

'Promise?'

'Promise.'

Dinner was a celebration, led by Clive. I was the maid of honour, best man and I felt like the vicar for a bit, but that soon passed. The other diners were the congregation, and Estelle's mother and father were the bell-ringers, the outside caterers and a sour old couple who stood at the gate muttering 'don't think they'll last long'. When you look at some people, and then you look at their parents, sometimes it's hard to believe. On my way to the dining room, I passed Estelle, who told me to 'watch my arse'. I told her that there wasn't much left of my arse to watch. When I looked at her I got the buzz at the root, I got creeping in the palms of my hands, and it was difficult to keep my hands off. I pinched her waist as I left her, I smiled at her mother in the dining room, who said, 'Will you be sitting at Mr Nobert's table?'

'You bet,' I said.

Clive stood up when he saw me, Mother kissed my cheek, I sat down carefully, and a glass of champagne was poured. I watched the bubbles foam and settle, then Clive said, 'Here's to us,' and he raised his glass.

'Surf's up,' I said.

'Cheers,' said Mother, and after she'd leant across and patted my shoulder, we drank together.

It was hot in the dining room. A faint smell of sweat mingled with the wafts of meat and vegetables from the kitchen; men sat in shirt-sleeves with their jackets hanging on the backs of their chairs, while their women shone and cast anxious, happy or lost looks around the room. Estelle's mother slammed my starter down in front of me. I thanked her, she didn't say a thing, I grinned at Clive. 'Something you said,' he said, 'or did?'

'Maybe,' I said, and I finished my first glass of champagne. He poured another and said, 'Plenty more where that came from,' and held his glass up.

Champagne's a good buzz. It breaks into the glass like a fairy's wave, it sprays your face with a mist of bubbles, people in the dining room who aren't drinking it look towards you and wonder what's up. The starter was a slice of melon with a cherry on it. The cherry sat there like a big nipple. When I picked it up and popped it in my mouth, I swilled it around my mouth, stuck the tip of my tongue into the hole where the stone had been, forced my tongue through and split the fruit in two. Mother watched me and said, 'Still playing with your food?'

I swallowed. 'Yup,' I said.

'Doesn't Susan tell you off?'

'I'm too old to tell off,' I said.

Clive laughed. Other diners steadied their glasses and looked at him. 'Old age pension next, is it?'

'You know what I mean,' I said.

When Clive ate, he cut his food into little pieces, popped them into his mouth quickly, and chewed slowly. When he did things he did them with careful thought. He knew his talents and he knew his limits. He sipped his champagne, and watched our glasses. When they were half full, he refilled them and caught Estelle's mother's eyes. He pointed to the bottle and raised his eyebrows. She nodded, and two minutes later came with another bottle.

There was a feeling between Clive and Mother you could touch, and I had to drink two glasses to kill the idea that I was gate-crashing something. Whenever their eyes met, you heard the messages they were passing. There was electricity in the air, and moisture. Light and dampness, a dull ache in my buttocks, the main course was a choice of fish or chicken.

I don't eat fish. Any creature that can get around without legs is alright with me; also, I'm afraid I might sweat a fishy smell in the sea, and they'll know what I've been doing. In Hastings, there's a man who owns a tropical-fish shop. I was in there once, and he was eating chips out of the paper. A customer came in and said, 'You're not eating . . .' and the customer mouthed '. . . fish and chips?' The shopkeeper shook his head and said, 'Never in front of the stock.' Fish have brains the size of beans, but why should they have anything bigger? They don't have much to think about, but what they do think about is important. Keep the scales shiny, don't envy, don't overeat. The stars cannot be torn down because there are no stars, the gills go without thinking. Only two South American countries do not have borders with Brazil. What are they? Fish's brains are not full of useless information. How do I know that? Clive said something to Mother, and she said, 'No, that's poppycock.'

I said, 'Do you know what poppycock means?'

'No, dear,' she said. She squinted at me. My glass was full again.

'It's from the Dutch,' I said. 'Pappekak.'

'And what does that mean?'

I looked at my food. I had chicken, roast potatoes, carrots and peas. 'I'll tell you later,' I said.

'Oh,' she said, knowingly.

'Ecuador and Chile,' I said.

'I beg your pardon?'

'Ecuador and Chile are the only South American countries that don't have borders with . . .'

'Brazil,' said Clive.

'Correct!' I said, and I patted his shoulder.

'I was there last year,' he said. 'It's an incredible place.'

'Is that where you built the hospital?' said Mother.

He laughed again. 'I didn't build it! I was helping to set up a unit, that's all.'

'You're too modest.'

'Modesty's got nothing to do with it.'

Mother turned to me and said, 'Listen to him.'

'You don't have to,' he said.

I smiled, but didn't say anything. I was feeling strange now, overcome and pissed. When I chewed my food, I seemed to chew for ever, my buttocks throbbed gently, the smells in the dining room could have drowned a bat. Estelle's mother threw the odd glance in our direction; our eyes met twice, and both times I felt the hairs on the back of my neck go up. I could tell what she thought, and see the size of her warnings. I imagined her wrestling boars in mud, and I imagined her fighting bears in the forest. She was big and she was efficient. The chicken was well-cooked, the potatoes had crunchy bits on them. The champagne was so good that after four glasses I was ready to take all my clothes off and pretend I was a teapot. 'So!' Clive said suddenly, 'Here's to us!' He raised his glass and beamed at Mother. They'd been talking about something, I don't remember what. Mother picked up her glass and said 'Us,' and chinked with his. They both looked at me, then at my glass. I looked at my glass, then at them, then I picked up my glass and chinked too. 'To us!' I shouted, and I laughed. 'A happy conclusion. Happiness all round.'

'Cheers!' said Clive.

'Cheers,' said Mother. She sipped, put down her glass and took out a handkerchief. Tears were forming in the corners of her eyes. 'I'm sorry,' she said, and she dabbed them. 'I couldn't cry for years and now look at me. I'm too happy . . .'

'Good for you,' said Clive.

'You can't be too happy,' I said.

Clive smiled.

'But I feel guilty too,' she said, and she blew her nose. 'Why me?'

'Don't think like that. Think "why not me?" It's high time you had your share.' Clive picked up her hand and kissed it. She sniffed. 'Crying's good for you.'

'Yeah.' I lifted my glass to her. 'Cry all you want, Mum,' I said, and I scratched my nose.

She stared at me for a moment, unblinking, then cried even more, wailing in her seat. Other diners looked up to watch, Clive stood up and held her shoulders. Estelle's mother came over like a chicken, clucking and flapping around, reassuring other people, poking her face in their food, making her way to our table. She kept her distance, and her hands together. 'Is madam well?' she said.

What does it look like? Estelle's mother had puckered lips and this daft concerned look on her face, and my God I hope this doesn't get around.

'Nothing to worry about,' said Clive, and he started to lead Mother away.

My food tasted sour.

'Come along, Di,' said Clive, and he ushered her out of the dining room and up the stairs with no trouble and no fuss. I stood up to watch them go; when I moved to follow them, Clive turned and waved me back, then gave the thumbs up. So I sat down again, and while the other diners returned to their food, leaning towards their plates and talking about us out of the sides of their mouths, I poured myself another glass of champagne.

When I got back to my room, I was flying. The champagne had taken a very light hold of my legs, and lifted them for me as I walked. It had given my arms a floaty, sinky, floaty feeling, and I could count up to at least six. I prayed for Mother, lay on the bed, took deep breaths, and shut my eyes.

Someone had taken the room next door. I heard them walk from the window to the bed, and then lay down quietly. I was naked, my clothes were in a pile on the floor, the air was suffocating. My skin crept and tingled, and every thought I had flashed through my brain at the speed of light. My mother's tears. Memories of Supertubes, anticipation of Estelle, the low pressure building and the coming storm. Mr Zog's Sex Wax. Original. Never spoils. The best for your stick. A variety of flavours, but don't try to eat it. Estelle knocked, I said, 'Yeah?', the bed in the next room creaked, Estelle came in, looked down my body and said 'Good Evening.' I stretched and said, 'When do we dance?' 'Now,' she said, and she kicked her shoes off. They arced across the room and fell down by the windows.

We drank a glass of wine together, she with her clothes on, me naked. 'Heard there was a fuss in the dining room,' she said. 'How is your Mum?'

'A fuss?' I said. 'Is that what it was?'

'It's what it was called. My old man reckoned she was having a breakdown.'

'Did he?'

'Yeah.'

'And what the hell does he know?' I said. 'I don't think he was even there.'

'I think he was . . .'

'One of these people who's an expert at everything, is he?'

'That's about it,' she said, 'but not as expert as me.' She laughed at me, and the laugh was exactly like a threat. Not a violent threat, more one loaded with fun.

'Or me.'

'You,' she said, and she dripped some wine into my navel and sucked it out. I tried to unbutton her blouse, but couldn't. She said, 'Expert, are you, or just pissed?' and did it. Then she sat on me. It was all big, big music; I was the mouth and she was the saxophone, and every note I blew echoed in my heart.

That night was slow and sticky. The heat clung and would not let go. We moved carefully, I kept her hands away from my buttocks, and let her do my waist instead. She's a strong woman, and shifted me around. I let it happen, I listened to the champagne swill backwards and forwards in my stomach, as the alcohol organised a restructuring of my mind and Estelle balanced her nipples on mine. I slapped the sides of her buttocks and watched the flesh ripple towards me. She told me to 'watch it', and started up long, soft lunges at me, arching her back and sweeping her hair across my face, then back, lifting her arms above her head, then down again, up again, the bed groaning, the person in the next room opening his windows, stepping on to the balcony and lighting a cigarette. I listened for the sea, but heard nothing. I put my hands on Estelle's waist. I kneaded her flesh, I leant forward and sucked some of it into my mouth. The person on the balcony creaked the boards, the curtains hung like damp rags. Estelle moaned softly, and I began to gurgle. Our noises harmonised, our flesh slapped together, it stuck and pulled away, sweat dropped from her forehead on to my lips. I licked it, it was fresh and salty, one of her breasts slapped the side of my face, then the other. I closed my eyes and stars burst in my head. Planets were born and then they died, it was death by unusual vegetable, it was a sea of flames. Asbestos surfboards and blisters on the soles of my feet. I had a pain in my head but I loved it; I opened my mouth and filled it with hair. I was awake and I was dreaming, and a piece of my heart grew larger than my life.

ELEVEN

In the morning the air was fresher, the clouds were moving and there was a tight edge to the atmosphere. I got up early, stood on the balcony and scratched. When I looked down, I saw Clive crossing the car park. He had his big hat on his head. I shouted down, and he called back, 'Fancy a stroll?'

'Coming,' I said. I threw some water on my face, brushed my teeth, grabbed some clothes and met him five minutes later.

The sea was beginning to chop, the cliff path was damp, the hotel sat quietly below us. When I looked down at it, I saw Estelle's mother come from the kitchen door and drop some rubbish in a bin. She looked at the sky but not at us, we turned a corner and left the hotel behind, and I said 'How's Mother?'

'Fine,' he said. 'She got a little overheated, that's all. There wasn't any air last night, was there?' He banged his chest. 'It's better today. Much better. You can breathe.'

'Yeah.'

'And she wasn't used to the drink. I think we all had too much, actually.' He smiled at me. 'But that's not a bad thing to do, once in a while, is it?'

'You're the doctor,' I said.

'Not that sort of doctor.' We crossed a stile, and took a path that led towards the cliff edge. 'But I know what I see, and I think I know your mother. Of course,' he said, and we slowed our pace, 'when you called her Mum that took the lid off it. Only to be expected though. When she went to bed she couldn't stop saying it herself. You never called her Mum before?'

'No.'

'Why not?'

I shrugged. 'She was never really a Mum; other kids had them. She was always Mother. It didn't mean I didn't love her any less, anything like that . . .'

'No.'

'. . . it just happened.'

'It meant a lot to her,' he said.

'Good.'

'And then you did something else, scratched your nose or something, and that clinched it . . .'

'I scratched my nose?'

'Exactly like your father used to, apparently.'

'Oh . . .'

'She said it was like sitting with a ghost. She loved it but it frightened her at the same time. She was very frightened, almost hysterical.'

'She thought I was his ghost yesterday, in St Ives, and half an hour later, I thought I heard him whistling in the car. "Bess, you is my woman now".'

'Gershwin?'

'You know it?'

'Indeed.'

'Dad could whistle like a bird.'

We came to the edge of the cliff. We stood there. Gulls were flying below us, crying across the sea, swooping towards the waves and pulling out of their dives with a foot to go, lashing at the water with their legs. The morning light was the colour of flesh, the clouds bowled towards us like thighs and calves. I said, 'A couple of days ago, all I wanted was to stay with her, to have her stay with me. We had all this catching up to do, but now . . .' The clouds filled and billowed, building up to big grey hammer-heads. A low, growling, weeping rumble of thunder rolled across the sea. '. . . I see her with you, and I know I can't.'

'You can't what?'

'Expect it.'

'She loves you very much,' he said.

'I know.'

'But it's not your job to make her mind up for her, and it's not mine either. She's special to you and she's special for me, but that means nothing if *she* doesn't feel that she's special.'

Special is one of those words – like 'butter' – that sounds meaningless if you say it enough times. I smiled at Clive. I think I must have looked touched. 'She is,' I said.

'As I said.'

'As you bloody well said,' I said.

We were at the very edge. A hundred feet below, awkward waves slammed against a pair of black pinnacle rocks, rose again and crashed on to a tiny, inaccessible beach. Patches of weed rose and fell in the swell, spindrift was blown in fine diagonal and climbing lines. The birds cried and cried. My stomach rumbled. The image of a rack of hot toast, a pat of butter and a large jar of marmalade rose in my mind. He said, 'She can only make her own mind up. Whatever she wants.'

'Yeah,' I said, 'I know. But don't you think that what she wants is the last thing we want?'

'What are you talking about?'

'You know . . .'

'No,' he said, 'I don't. Tell me.'

'Clapham Junction.'

He stared at the drop and the waves, and swept his hair out of his eyes. 'That was then,' he said, 'this is now, and this is different.'

'Is it?'

I waited for an answer as the wind buffeted us, and the sea did not give up. 'Yes,' he said, eventually, but the word came out weakly, dropped at our feet and lay in the grass, quivering.

At breakfast, Mother smiled weakly, drank two cups of coffee and ate a piece of dry toast. She wasn't wearing any make-up, and her hair was tied back severely. She looked ten years older, and when she spoke, she sounded it. When Clive suggested a drive to Cape Cornwall, maybe some lunch in a pub, she shook her head and said, 'I think I'll stay put this morning. Maybe this afternoon; I'm feeling a bit woozy.' She looked at Clive's bacon and eggs, and paled.

I said, 'Did you sleep alright?'

She looked at her coffee, then directly at me. Her eyes grew too big for their lids, and I thought they might pop out. She rubbed her lips with the side of a finger, and her nostrils started up this minute quivering. Her eyes bored into me, her breathing quickened, she was puffing. Her nose was as red and shiny as a cherry and her hair, pulled tightly away from her forehead, revealed masses of tiny veins. Her blood was going and her ears twitched. I was scared; I waited for her head to explode and I wondered if I'd scratched my nose again. She whispered, 'Yes, thank you,' from behind the finger, picked up a spoon and began stirring her coffee, staring at it as if her life depended on it.

I looked at Clive and he looked at me, and Estelle's mother and father looked at me. They stood by the kitchen door and said things to each other. They planned the odd plan and congratulated themselves on it. They made sure my toast was cold before I got it, and they had left cheaper marmalade on the table. Sweet stuff with rind like bootlaces; I was picking some out, turning it over on the end of my knife, when

Mother dabbed her lips with her napkin, stood up and quietly left the table. 'In fact,' she said, 'I think I'll go up now. I really do feel quite peculiar.'

'I'll come up too,' said Clive.

'No dear,' she said, 'finish your breakfast.' She reached out and put her hand on my shoulder, but she didn't look at me. 'And you . . .' – she said 'you' as if she didn't know who I was – '. . . don't bolt your food', and the dining room was suddenly shaken by a clap of thunder, and lightning flashed across the horizon. Fat drops of rain began to fall, banging against the dining-room windows like nails. Estelle's father ran outside and collected some ashtrays from the patio tables and tilted the patio chairs against the tables. Clive waited five minutes, then excused himself, dabbed at the corners of his mouth with a napkin, and went upstairs. I watched another flash before showing Estelle's mother a full set of teeth, and the cupped palms of my hands.

I knocked on Mother's door, and Clive opened it. She was lying in bed, propped up by pillows, facing the windows. Her hair was sweaty, lying on her head like worms. Her eyes were translucent and heavily lidded. She was clenching a handkerchief in one hand and the bedclothes with the other. I sat on the bed, laid my hand on the bulge made by her right knee and said, 'What happened? You were so happy last night, and I don't think you drunk that much.'

'I'm alright,' she wheezed, 'really. A morning in the quiet and I'll be OK again.'

'Please,' I said, 'you're talking to me. Duncan. You can't say anything I can't take, not after all this time.' I tapped my chest. 'Hard as nails,' I said, 'and twice as sharp.'

She squeezed my hand. 'I know, dear.'

'You believe what I told you yesterday?'

'When was that?'

'Before dinner. I'm not stupid. Canada and all that. You're getting a life.'

'What's that mean?'

I looked at Clive. 'I know what's best for you.'

'Do you?' She looked at me, then at him. 'Do either of you?' Her voice took on a hard top. 'When I'm with one of you I'm thinking how lucky I am, but I'm also thinking that I want to be with the other. I wonder; am I ready for either of you?' Clive took a step forward, and sat on the bed with us. He held her other hand. 'Sometimes,' she said, 'I think I'm going to snap.'

'You won't do that,' said Clive.

'No,' I agreed.

'I really think I might.'

'Mother,' I said, 'if anyone's going to snap, it'll be the manager. He makes you look as fit as a fiddle.'

'The manager?' she said.

'Of the hotel.'

'Oh . . .' she said, and she smiled weakly, '. . . yes. First he has to put up with me, then you're chasing his daughter round the place.'

'Who said I was doing that?'

She tapped the side of her nose, and winked. 'Do cats howl at night? Do dogs bark?'

'Ha!' I said.

Another clap of thunder, a flash of lightning and rain began to fall steadily. 'I think Cape Cornwall might be off,' said Clive.

'No!' said Mother. 'Go. Please. Don't let me stop you.' She smiled. 'If it's the last thing you do for me . . .'

'It won't be that,' said Clive.

'No,' and Mother patted his hand, 'of course it won't be.'

I went to Sennen and surfed the storm. Wipeout. Do the

obvious, Mother, please. Degrees of happiness do not exist. A rabbit will never be a dog, and five potatoes don't make ten carrots. Bridges through the air, waves in the barrel of a gun, bang, bang, bang, all in my brain, round and round, giving me such grief. I swore I wished I'd never come down to Cornwall, I swore it was the only thing I could have done. Bang, bang, bang, big ideas, small thoughts, Estelle's hips, Mother's hand, Clive's head. My head cleared when I entered the water and pushed away from the shore. I was singing 'December' in my head, and when the first wave smashed over me, I began to shout it: '. . . after long years in the monkeyhouse, I'm ready for the storm, let them throw all their cannonballs, let all their strongmen come . . .' and I kicked and kicked against the swell.

The surf was angry and impossible, as wild and unpredictable as cats in ranked invisible cages. As I paddled through it, it hit and scratched, snarled and fanged. The rain fell steadily, the clouds were deep and very dark, towering over the sea. Spindrift flew with the rain, water came at me from every direction; I paddled with my eyes almost shut, looking out at the storm through slots.

I was fifty yards out when a clap of thunder burst directly above me, shivering the water; lightning flashed immediately, illuminating the bowling clouds with massive balls of light. For a moment, the sea shone luminous, the yawning pits between the sets of waves appeared to flatten and their crests calmed. The illumination held on to itself, then quickly went. It took its comfort with it, the rain fell vertically, horizontally and diagonally, it hit me from every angle and in every way. I forced the board along, each stroke of my paddle took me into wilder water, waves with big frothy lips that broke as they formed and broke into each other as they died. More thunder exploded, three more balls of lightning burnt the outlines of all the clouds on to the back of my eyes. I forgot, I didn't remember. There was no Mother, no Clive, not much of Estelle, no university in a fortnight's time. I was alone, I turned to face the shore when I was a hundred yards out, and counted the waves as they rolled towards me.

Three had come and gone when I dropped in on one that appeared to have more length than the others. It was already breaking at different points when I started to ride; it was an angled wall of foam, nothing predictable about it, but once I was up and shooting, cutting back all the time to keep critical and stable, I felt safe. My right foot started to hum, and my left began to tap in time. A slow piece with tears at the roots, music of protection, coming from beneath the sea. I held the wave for as long as I could, I took it to the shore, where it broke on the sand with a frustrated slap.

As I paddled out again, the rain began to harden, falling in desperate sheets from the densest, angriest clouds. They were criminal things, low and sweeping, with glowering faces and deep, gravelly voices. Each one followed the next without thought or question; another roll of thunder shivered the waves, the waves burst over me. I struggled to hold my line. Head to the waves, nose of the board cutting at the right angle, mouth closed.

The water began to bang chords on my head, running scales up and down my back. The paddling was hard. Once the board slipped from beneath me, caught a break of its own and ripped me to the right, dragging me parallel with the beach and kicking me against the bottom. I yanked the leash and the board snapped back at me, over my head and down behind me. I pulled it in, flattened it with my stomach and paddled on.

More lightning ripped across the sky and flashed along the crests of every wave. It was fat and yellow, and blasted the cliffs that rose above the cove; I got seventy yards out, and sat up on my board. Line-up. Stuff was breaking all around me, the swell heaved, the rain covered the surface of the water with patches of dark and light; I breathed slow and evenly.

I had waited for a minute when I saw what I thought was a heavy cloud, closer than any other, but then it disappeared. I looked for it, I shaded my eyes against the rain, my board threatened to leave me again. I turned to pull it back. I yanked it between my legs and gripped with my thighs. There was a fast and sharp crack of thunder above me, and the echo of this slammed into my spine and skinned my feet. I put my fingers in my ears and shook my head, then turned again and the heavy cloud was no cloud, it was rising behind me, a hump of steaming, manic water, as tall as a building and as busy as all the people who would be in that building. Hundreds of people, the lights are on in the rooms they work in, and their telephones are ringing. My telephone was ringing, and when I picked it up someone on the other end said 'watch your arse'. Estelle. She had thighs like surf, and firm, round hips. I started to paddle madly, kicking and scrabbling to catch the hump, which had begun to cast a shadow over me. It was as dark as dusk, the rain fell in a solid wall, I locked my arms straight, tucked my feet up, pushed and was suddenly picked up by the hump that boiled above and around me, flattening the churning waves in front. I concentrated on balance, I thought about the shore, I concentrated on my upper body, I held my line for five seconds, and it was a good five seconds too. I found a perfect shelf of clean water that cradled me and did not let me go, but then the hump began to swivel on its axis, and I began to go with it.

At first, I thought the whole world was turning. A clap of thunder was followed by a spit of lightning that cut the western sky from top to bottom, but then the western sky was the eastern sky, and I was pointing out to sea. I couldn't work out how I'd ended up that way, but before I had the chance to think, I was pointing to shore again, and my board was facing me, standing vertically in front of me, blocking the view. I saw the big Hot Tuna on its nose, and another decal I had put there. Surfers Against Sewage. Surfers Against the Communist Master of Disease. I opened my mouth to say something to my board, but then it was gone, flying over my head, and the leash went taut. I saw it angle to my right and I went with it, into the heart of the hump. I thought my leg was going to be ripped from its socket, a pain filled my foot. Boiling heat ripped from my head to my toes, then I was cold and my life was very dark.

Under the water, in this freak wave, everything raged but was very quiet. The white shape I saw was my board, and the flexible thing was my arm. I tucked my leg up and reached for the leash's cuff; I released it, floated for a second, and then I sank.

I hit the bottom hard, smashing my back on a slab of rock. I pushed back up, fighting the pressure and the current, the pain and the water in me. I was filling and I was stinging, I was thrashing and caught being the idiot. I was afraid but most of all I was lonely. I wanted to be with someone, anyone, a flight of arms. Flesh and hair, water and warmth. I felt the air as it left my lungs, a curtain of bubbles rose in front of my eyes, and the touch of death fingered my face. Its bony fingers circled my mouth, parted my lips and poked inside. They ran along my teeth, and when the bubbles cleared I watched my mother come towards me in the water. She was weeping and screaming, holding Dad's hands and telling me the last thing I wanted to hear. Her skin was grey and peeling, her hair was floating away from her head, and all around her eels were gathering, sliming in fat and awful gangs. Mother's screams began to fade, and soon she was muttering at me, one word running into the next until all the words sounded as one. 'Release me,' she said, 'release me.' My poor mother. With my last breath I said, 'I can't do that,' and another flood of bubbles burst out of my mouth, her image floated away, I pushed with all my strength, kicked my legs and surfaced behind the Communist Master of Disease as it cruised towards the shore.

It had left a calm wake, but boiling water was filling up behind me; I struck out for the beach, freestyling with long and wretched strokes. I kept an eye out for my board but it was nowhere. I kept an eye out for Estelle but she hadn't parked by the Beetle, she hadn't brought an umbrella. I watched for Mother; she was resting and recovering. I flopped into the shallows, hauled myself on to the sand and lay on my stomach. The rain didn't stop, the clouds didn't lighten and the thunder rolled off the sea and into Cornwall. I gagged and spat, and fingered my suit. Strips of rubber were hanging off the back, and I was bleeding. There was hell in my head and a terrific bouncing all around, as if the land was made of the sea and was returning to it.

TWELVE

I lay in the storm, on the beach, for half an hour. Then I sat up and watched the surf for my board, but it didn't come back. It was out there, it had the leash attached, but it was gone. I'd surfed all the waves on that board, from St Agnes and the power sets of Chapel Porth, to Hengistbury Head and the Isle of Wight. Four years on one board and I never dinged it once. Cry a little, die a little; once I thought I saw it, a white curve looping between the crests of two waves, but this was a gull, swooping towards a fish, and the gull rose into the sky. It flew over me, heading inland, screaming. I stripped off my wet-suit, wrapped myself in towels and sat in the car. I was angry and sad, my arse ached and my back burned. My face was bruised and I had a stinging cut over my left eye. I dabbed it with antiseptic, and then sat for the rest of the morning and half the afternoon, dozing off once, then coming round, dressing and driving to St Just. I sat in a café by the square, ate some sausage and chips, and drank two cups of tea. I was the only customer, and I sat by the window.

I watched a pair of old hippies as they parked their pick-up. They were hairy and wore pullovers the size of gardens, and baggy blue and pink trousers. One of them carried a baby slung in a length of material, the other had a string shopping-bag. They went to a supermarket, they held the door open for an old lady who was coming out, and then they disappeared inside.

God I ached from the top of my head to my feet, and where I bled, the blood stuck to my shirt. I put a finger to my face and touched the bruises. I winced, and the waitress came up to me. She said, 'You look like you could do with an aspirin.'

I shook my head.

'Paracetamol?'

'Thanks,' I said, 'but I'm alright.'

'What happened?'

'A conversation with Sennen.'

'You what?'

'I was surfing.'

She pointed outside. 'In that?'

I nodded and finished my tea. 'I caught this wave you wouldn't believe. The Communist Master of Disease.'

'You what?'

'That's what it's called. What I called it.'

'Are you soft in the head?'

'Probably,' I said.

'Definitely, more like,' she said, and she scooped up my empty plate and went to the kitchen.

The hippies came out of the supermarket, ran for their pick-up, tossed their bag of shopping in, then sat in the cab. They played with their baby for a bit, bouncing it up and down on their knees. I could see it smiling, the hippies were smiling; one of them took some apples out of the bag and they ate them.

The rain didn't stop, and nor did the wind, though as the afternoon died, the thunder faded to a distant rumble and the lightning disappeared. The low pressure moved slowly, the weathermen were right, and they wore the clothes they wore. There was nothing wrong with that, and I didn't blame them for anything. Cardigans or smart suits; as long as their maps were right, I wasn't complaining. I touched my eye again and watched the hippies drive away. Their exhaust was hanging off and they backfired out of the square, down the road to Cape Cornwall. I had another cup of tea, passed another quiet hour, and then drove slowly back to the River Cove Hotel.

The rain did not stop. When I parked, I sat in the Beetle and listened to it beating on the roof. I'd been there for a couple of minutes when Clive appeared from the hotel, ran down the steps and splashed across the car park towards me. He banged on the passenger window, I opened the passenger door, he squeezed himself into the car, shook the rain from his hair and said, 'Have you seen her?'

'Who?'

'Diana.' He ran his hand through his hair and wiped it on his trousers. He was breathing heavily, panting like a dog. 'Your mother,' he said, 'who'd you think?'

'Well . . .' I said, and '. . . no.' The back of my neck prickled. 'Why?'

He looked through the windscreen, he looked at his watch, he looked through the windscreen again and slapped his forehead with the palm of his hand. 'Idiot,' he whispered.

'Who's an idiot?'

'I am. I went to Cape Cornwall, had lunch on the cliffs, and when I got back, she was gone.' He took out a handkerchief, wiped his forehead and said, 'I should never have left her on her own; I'm afraid for her . . .' He turned to look at me, saw my bruises, squinted at them and said, 'My God! What happened to you?'

'I was surfing.'

'Surfing?'

'Yeah. I lost my board.'

'And almost your head, by the looks of it.' He put out a hand to touch my face, I moved back. 'You want me to clean you up?'

'It's nothing. But Mother. She's gone where?'

He shook his head, and looked through the windscreen again. 'Just gone.'

I looked at my watch. 'How long?'

'Three, maybe four hours. The manager said she'd told him she was only going to be half an hour.' He pointed out of the window. 'Up to the top and back again. I went up myself an hour ago, but there was no sign of her.'

'Maybe she decided to go on for a bit.'

'In this? I could hardly see where I was going, and the path was mud. It's treacherous.'

I looked at the rain. Maybe she wanted to get wet, she wanted to feel uncomfortable and threatened. It's how I feel, and how I enjoy myself. I said, 'Did she take a torch?'

'I don't know. Why?'

'She was out the night I arrived; Estelle said she'd been out every night, and she always took a torch.'

Clive opened the door, and rain blew into the car. 'I'll give her another half an hour, then I'm off again.'

'OK,' I said, 'I'll be with you.'

He squinted at my face again and said, 'Sure you don't want a plaster for that?'

I touched the cut. The blood had dried, and the pain was just a dull ache. 'No,' I said, 'I'll be alright.'

Clive held the door-handle for a moment, said, 'If you say so,' and then dashed across the car park, up the stone steps and into the hotel. I followed; I tried to run but my legs wouldn't go. I stumbled into the reception. Estelle was behind the desk, the door slammed shut behind me and she said, 'Duncan! Bloody hell! What happened to your face?'

'I got caught.'

'By what?'

'A wave.'

She came from behind the desk, and touched my forehead. 'It looks bad.'

'You should see my back,' I said.

'Why?'

'That's worse.'

'You want me to give it a rub?' She put her hand on my chest, over my heart, and made a circle with her fingers.

'I don't think so,' I said. 'I don't want to lose what skin I've got left.'

'That bad?'

'Yeah,' I said, as her old man came from his office and stood behind the desk. I looked towards him, then back at Estelle. She looked towards him, and he said, 'What I'm going to do is this. I'm going to tot up all the odd minutes you take off in the day, and then at the end of the week I'll give you the total and you can work the extra on Sundays.'

'What?' she said.

'Yes. I think that's a very good idea, don't you?' Her father smoothed his hair with his hands, and smiled an idiot grin. 'Maybe then you'll start to understand that this isn't a holiday for you.'

'Start to understand?' she said, her hands on her hips.

'Exactly,' he said.

'I finished understanding that ages ago.'

'It didn't stick though, did it?' He jabbed one of his stubby little fingers at her head.

Estelle turned her face away from him, as if she'd just been slapped.

'When I represented England, we played as a team, and that's how I want us to work here.'

'He doesn't want to know about you and England.'

The bloke looked at me, then back at Estelle. 'I'm not talking to him, or for his benefit . . .'

'You could have fooled me.'

'It's you I'm worried about,' he said.

'Worried now, are you?'

'Yes. And you should be too. Your Mother and I have just . . .'

'Excuse me,' I said, 'but that reminds me. I've got to go and find my mother.'

'Have you?' said Estelle's father, and he squinted at me with his thin eyes. For a middle-aged man he had very grey hair, and a strange way of standing. Estelle stripped me naked with her eyes, and applied a deep and cooling lotion to my wounds.

'Yes,' I said to him, and I put my hand out to Estelle. 'Thanks very much,' I said to her. She winked at me and licked her lips. I got this sudden buzz in my stomach that ran down to my groin and zapped it. I enjoyed the feeling and then I went upstairs. I ran a tepid bath, peeled my clothes off, climbed in carefully and soaked for ten minutes. Then I sat on the bed and phoned Susan. She told me off for not phoning before, and said that Marcus had bet I wouldn't phone at all.

'How much?' I said.

'He didn't bet money,' she said, 'just a drink.'

'So,' I said, 'what's yours?'

She ignored that, and said, 'So how is she?'

'Not back from a walk.'

'Oh . . .'

'Clive's doing his nut. It's pissing down, terrible weather, so we're off to look for her in a minute.'

'Oh dear.'

'Yeah,' I said. 'I'm afraid for her.'

'Why?'

'She's confused, having trouble deciding what to do. Sometimes I think she's going to do something stupid.'

'What does stupid mean?'

'You know . . .'

'No, I don't know,' said Susan in her steady, matter-of-fact voice. 'Tell me.'

'Did she ever say anything to you about Clapham Junction?'

'Oh . . .'

'Did she?' my voice was up.

'Yes.'

'Well,' I said, almost angry now, but trying not to show it. 'She gets this look in her eyes, as if she's about to give up, that's what really scares me.'

'She needs help . . .'

'We're doing all we can,' I said.

'I'm sure you are, but maybe she should see a professional.'

'Clive's a professional.'

'But I don't think he's the right sort, is he?'

'No, but . . .'

'I don't suppose she'd see the right sort in any case. She can be very stubborn.'

'I know,' I said.

'She always has been. When she was a little girl, she was terrible, she never let things drop . . .'

'Did you know,' I said, 'that she was talking about going to Canada?'

There was silence.

'With Clive?' I said.

Silence.

'Susan?'

'Yes,' she said, quietly. 'I think she did say something about it . . .'

'When I first saw her, it was definite. She was leaving on Monday with Clive.'

'What's he like?'

'Big,' I said.

'Big?'

'Yeah. Anyway. Then she started wondering if it was such a good idea. I asked her to come and live with me in Exeter.'

'And?'

'Then I thought why should I? It's her life, I don't want her to think she owes me anything. Canada's a long way to go, but at least I'd know where she was. It's the knowing bit . . .'

'Yes . . .'

'So I told her. Make your mind up, please yourself, for God's sake, but be happy.'

'That was kind of you,' she said.

'Susan,' I said, 'whatever happens, she is my mother. I don't think kindness has got much to do with it . . .'

'Don't be so stupid.'

'Anyway,' I said, and there was a knock on the door. 'That'll be Clive now.'

'Oh,' said Susan, 'OK. You'd better go. Phone again.'

'I will.' I got up and opened the door.

'And love to your mother. Tell her I want to see her next.' Clive tiptoed into the bedroom. Watching this was like watching a dream horse drink sherry.

'OK,' I said. 'Bye.'

'Bye,' said Susan.
'Fit?' said Clive.
'Ready.'

THIRTEEN

I didn't have a coat, so Clive leant me his spare. It was knee-length on him but touched the ground on me. My hands were a quarter way up the sleeves, and the collar covered half my chest. It was like wearing a cave.

He also leant me a hat; I had to pack it with newspaper to make it fit. He wore heavy boots and a trilby, and carried a torch. When we walked through reception, Estelle's father glowered as we passed. We slapped our keys down on the desk, and Clive said 'Good evening,' to him in a civilised way, and I raised my eyebrows. Estelle's father shuffled uneasily. His glory days were gone, and all he had left were sad memories. How do men like him have daughters? Why? When? I wanted to kick him where he stood, but I left it. Leave a man like him till later, or not at all.

As we headed up the cliff path it was growing dark; the ground was greasy, the rain had not eased. We passed the bench and crossed the grassy plateau, then took the corner and left the hotel behind us. We climbed quickly to the top of the cliff, and at the summit, Clive stopped, cupped his hands over his lips and shouted 'Diana!'

The word was ripped from his mouth by the wind and disappeared; we stood still for a minute, craning towards the gloom, but there was no reply. So we walked on, taking a track that snaked away in a darkening, grey ribbon. One careful foot after another, our arms stretched out for balance and our tongues held against the back of our teeth. A sudden gap in the clouds let in the watery light of a dying moon, then it was gone.

Clive's coat was heavy, a piece of newspaper slipped out of the hat. I tucked it back in, wiped my face and touched my bruises. They were coming up nicely, big red bumps on my cheeks and neck. I looked to sea, but I couldn't see the board, and when I looked at the sky, it whined back at me. My feet slipped, I put my arms out to steady myself, and bent at the knees. 'Alright?' said Clive. He was leading the way, and stopped to watch me sliding towards him.

'No problem.'

He put out a hand and helped me up. I brushed myself down, and he yelled 'Diana!' again.

No reply.

'Mother!'

Nothing.

'Maybe she walked in the back door as we went out the front,' he said. 'For all we know, at this very minute, she's running a nice hot bath and sipping a cup of tea.'

'Maybe,' I said, 'but I don't think so.'

'No,' he said quietly. 'I couldn't sit around and do nothing. If she's hurt . . .'

'She won't be,' I said, and gripped his arm. It was solid but I felt it give as I held him. 'We're doing the right thing.'

'I know that,' he said, 'I just hope we'll be able to laugh about it in the morning.'

'I can't laugh at anything in the morning,' I said.

'No?' he said. 'I enjoy the mornings. The best time of the day; it's when my brain works properly. After midday, it starts to let me down.'

'It's the other way round with me.'

'Your mother's boy,' he said.

'Eh?'

'Diana's the same; just the same.'

An abandoned engine-house stood in a field below us. The old chimney stood against the sky like a big finger, clouds raged over, and the wind whistled around the crumbling brickwork. For thousands of years, tin and copper was mined in Cornwall, but now not a single mine is working, all fucked by cheap imports. The one we approached was ringed by rusted barbed wire and broken poles at angles, and signs: DANGER. DEEP SHAFTS. KEEP OUT. Red letters on a white background; the place was haunted by the rhythmic thump of the old pump, the shouts of men, the gossip of waiting women, crying children and the smell of boiled turnips. We straddled the wire, crossed some grassy humps and came to the circle of stones that marked the edge of the shaft. This opened into utter darkness, as deep as the sea, like a vertical stone wave, a barrelling death tube into nothing. The sound of dripping water echoed, we stood in the lee of a crumbling wall and looked at each other. In the dusk, Clive's face looked grey and his hair looked darker than it is. I felt faint, and when our eyes met I could see him thinking what I was thinking. Our thought came from the place we had hidden it, it forced its way out and kicked its way down a short passage to bang on a door and shout. The worst feeling is not knowing, not knowing where someone is, or what has happened to them. What their head has told them, or the depths their eyes have sunk to. The mine-shaft was this feeling, it was all our fears in one terrible hole. I leant into it and yelled 'MUM!'

The word dropped from my mouth, bouncing against the sides of the shaft as it fell, rummaging in all the fissures and cracks, feeling the moss and damp, and then it echoed back at me:

'MUM!'

'MUM!'

Clive said, 'I don't think that's going to do any good.'

'I know.'

'If she jumped . . .' He pointed the torch at the muddy ground around the shaft, but then shook his head ' . . . but I don't think she's been here. I can't see any footprints.'

'What are those?'

'Ours.' He turned the torch off, and a crow squawked above us and exploded into flight. The moon flashed again and illuminated the side of the chimney and my hands in front of my face.

'God,' I said, and I looked back down the shaft. 'It gives me the creeps.'

'I was reading about this one,' said Clive. 'It goes down below the cliffs, then out under the sea.'

'Fuck.'

'Yes,' he said, 'that's about the strength of it.'

We walked on, quickening our pace. Whenever we came to a clump of weather-beaten shrubs, a piece of broken ground or a stretch of wall, he shone the torch, flashing it into the dark places. The rain had weakened and was beginning to fall as drizzle, the clouds were moving slower, and the dark was looming. Pendeen lighthouse began to swing its beam, warning of treacherous rocks. The regular pulse of light was a comfort, the only comfort. If you looked straight at it, it put spots behind your eyes. It illuminated the curtains of drizzle and cut a line across the sky. It attracted birds, they gathered on its parapets; Clive's torch swung in unison, across the path and down to a place where the path split. There was a stone marker here, and a small tree. We stood and looked in both directions. One path went up, climbing a steep, barren hill; the other went down, disappearing around a sharp corner towards the sea.

'What do you think?' I said. 'Which way did she go?'

Clive stared up, then pointed down. 'She'd rather sit on a lonely beach than climb a hill. She likes to stare at the sea, fingers through the sand, that sort of thing.' He nodded.

'Yes . . .' he said, ' . . . down. Come on.'

After the sharp corner, the path dropped steeply, almost falling towards the shore. It was narrow and overgrown with bushes and brambles, but people had been using it, there were footprints in the mud. There were also small birds in the bushes, and they started up a damp racket as we passed. The sea crashed below us, the crests of each wave lit by the blue, dusky and drizzly light, and then the Pendeen light, and then another glimpse of the moon, racing behind the clouds.

The bottom of the path was strewn with rocks and boulders. We picked our way around and over them, jumped some rock-pools and stood on the beach. It was pebbled, shaped like half a filling North Atlantic low, and shelved steeply to the sea. Waves pounded a low stack of offshore rocks, burst around them and washed on to the shore. The noise of the pebbles as they were drawn back, the crashing surf, the crying gulls above us; Clive shouted 'DIANA!' He cupped his mouth and shouted again, and we walked towards the back of the beach.

The cliffs were black and craggy. Clive washed them with the torch-beam, slowly passing it up and down. He called again, and I did too. He shone it at some roosting gulls and he shone it at a rotting lobster pot, and he shone it at a clump of grass growing in a fissure forty feet above us. We saw piles of weed hanging from low crevices, and some empty plastic bottles twinkled as the beam caught them. I looked at the cliff and saw it as a wave, and when I listened to the sea it sounded like rocks falling. I yelled 'MUM!' and no answer came, and the gulls laughed back at me. Clive was twenty yards away from me when he called 'Duncan!' and I ran to him.

He was shining the torch at a hole in the cliff. We walked towards it. The smell of salt and rotting weed was strong. I wiped my face with my sleeve and said, 'What do you think?'

'I don't know.' We were crouched down, and he was

pointing the beam inside. He stuck his head in, and when he said 'It looks big,' his voice boomed, echoing inside the cliff. It sounded as if the cliff was speaking. He called 'DIANA!' and crawled inside. I took my hat off, and a pile of sodden newspaper sat on top of my head. I put this in the hat, and followed.

We stood up inside the cave, and when Clive shone the torch, the beam hit the ceiling twenty feet above us. The sound of the sea seemed to come from miles away, drips of water echoed all around. It was freezing cold. I blew on my hands, and the breath floated into the torch-beam, and into the roof. There was a squeaking, and a rapid sound in the air. 'Bats,' said Clive, and the word boomed, snaking around and around the walls. The chamber was shaped like a bell, narrowing along one side to another hole. Clive pointed the torch and held my hand for a moment. 'Alright?' he said. His face was very close, and his breath smelt of peppermint.

'Yeah,' I said.

'Come on then. Let's see.'

'OK.'

The hole was the entrance to a corridor. This was narrow and curved gently to the left as it rose into the cliff. The floor was smooth and puddled; the torch-beam illuminated our path in a circle, lighting the ceiling, walls and floor. It was like being deeply tubed in a stone wave, settling slowly into its rhythm, waiting for the moment to pop out. Our footsteps echoed softly, my coat dragged behind me, and a trickle of perspiration ran down my back. It ran slowly, stopping at each knuckle of my spine until it reached the bottom and soaked away. I felt soaked away, I felt as old as the cave, and as cold, and my thoughts echoed as the drips of water echoed around us. Another bat flitted over our heads, turned a circle in the light of the torch and flew back the way it had come. Its wings brushed my face as it passed; I took out a handkerchief and mopped my forehead as Clive stopped, held up his hand and said, 'Can you smell that?'

I sniffed. 'Seaweed?' I said.

'No.' He sniffed.

'What?'

He walked on without answering.

The corridor straightened and levelled off, and then began to widen. Exactly like a tube ride, exactly like some terrible wave with the power to energise a dozen cities, the Communist Master of Disease's brother, a fossil wave with a heart of steel. Something you could be caught in and never killed by. As dangerous as Porthleven on a heavy day, jacking up out of nowhere. Ripping and turning without any warning at all; we popped out into a second chamber, and Clive said, 'It's in here.' He sniffed again, deeply.

'What's in here?' I said.

'Peau d'Espagne.'

'What?' I said.

'Your mother's favourite perfume,' he said.

I sniffed.

'Can you smell it?'

'Yeah,' I said.

'She's here.' He coughed, and the sound cracked high above us. He whispered, 'Diana?'

There was a sweet smell there, mingling with the salt and weed and the damp smell of the rocks.

'Diana?'

High above us, a hole in the roof let in the last of the day's light and threw a pale smear down the cave's walls. It caught a drip of water, then another, and one that fell on my head.

'Diana?'

There was a musical note in the air, made by the wind as it passed over the hole, and I heard the sound of a gull.

'Diana?'

Its cry was lonely and hungry and full of pain.

'Diana?' Clive swept the floor of the chamber with the torch-beam.

Stones were piled around the place, shingle lay in patches between them, and the walls were covered in green slime. Another drip hit my nose. It was freezing but felt hot.

'Diana? Are you there?'

As we moved, our footsteps made dull echoes, and my coat flapped like a damp tent. I shivered, said 'Mum?' and the sweeping light caught her.

She was sitting on a ledge of rock, raised up from the floor, directly beneath the hole of light but away from its direct smear. Clive ran to her, taking his coat off as he did, and he wrapped it around her shoulders. 'Diana,' he said, 'thank God!' He stroked her face and hair, his voice was soft and reassuring. 'What are you doing here? We were worried.'

She looked at him, her face lit by the torch. This made her look frightened and frightening at the same time. She said, 'I was just coming, but I couldn't leave.' She looked up and around. 'This is my little bolthole.'

'Your what?' I said.

'It's where I've been coming when I need to think.' She rummaged in a pocket and took out her torch. She shone it at her bag, a thermos of tea and a half-eaten packet of biscuits. 'How did you find me?'

'Followed our noses,' said Clive. 'Peau d'Espagne.'

'Ah,' she said, and she smiled weakly and tapped the side of her nose. 'You and your sense of smell.'

'We were very worried . . .'

'I'm sorry,' said Mother, 'but at least you can consider it worry well spent,' and she stood up, picked up her things and climbed down from the ledge.

'Why's that?' I said.

'Because I know what I'm going to do,' she said, and she

brushed past us and headed for the corridor. Her perfume was strong and it drifted around me, filling my nostrils.

'What's that?' I said, following, but she was hurrying away, and didn't answer.

FOURTEEN

I asked Mother again, and Clive asked her, but she would not tell us what she was going to do. She closed the windows, drew the curtains and locked the shutters, so no light escaped, or sound. She walked ahead of us all the way back to the hotel, and when we got there, went straight to her room. Clive and I stood in reception, and he asked me if I wanted a drink. We went to the bar and sat at a corner table.

Estelle's father ignored us for five minutes, then, as he passed us on his way back from another table, said 'What would you like?' out of the corner of his mouth, as if he was doing us a favour.

'Duncan?' said Clive.

'Whiskey,' I said.

'Two whiskies,' said Clive.

'Ice?' said Estelle's father.

'Don't even show it any,' said Clive, and I nodded in agreement. The man looked at us as if we were mad, then shuffled back to the bar. He rummaged noisily for some glasses, huffed and puffed as he fiddled with an optic, and scratched his head while he calculated the cost. When he brought them over, he banged them down on the table, crossed his arms and said, 'Two seventy.'

'Put them on my bill,' said Clive, 'would you?'

Estelle's father looked at him, huffed again, said, 'As you will,' and went back to the bar.

'What an unfortunate man,' said Clive, and he swilled his whiskey in the glass, then drank half of it in one.

'If he was made of chocolate, he'd eat himself,' I said.

'Ha!'

I picked up my glass and said, 'Surf's up.'

'Cheers,' he said, and then we sat in silence for five minutes.

Other guests in the bar burbled around us; some had maps and guidebooks opened out on tables in front of them, others were sitting back with their legs crossed, in conversation about the National Trust, the hotel food, the day's storm and a television programme about Hungarian fire-fighters in the Kuwaiti desert. Through the window, I watched sheets of drizzle as they blew across the car park and out to sea. Clive examined his fingernails, found some loose skin and began to pick at it. I said, 'As a doctor, what's the prognosis?'

'You only know the prognosis when you've diagnosed,' he said, 'and every time I think I've done that, I'm proved wrong.' He had another sip of whiskey. 'Your mother's not the sort of woman to take advice, however well meant. She has to work these things out for herself. She's a very strong woman, but weak too, a classic dichotomy. From a clinical point of view, she's endlessly fascinating . . .'

'Is that why you like her?'

'Love her,' he said.

'Love her . . .' I said, rolling the words.

'No,' he said, 'that's not the reason.'

'Why then?'

He finished his whiskey and waved Estelle's father over. He said to me, 'I don't know,' and to Estelle's father he said, 'Two more, please.' I finished mine in a gulp, and passed my glass to him. I smiled at him, my smile reaching from ear to ear and all over my body, so I imagined that I was one big smile, and I was pleased.

I lay lightly in my bed, the aches in my body whispered to each other through my veins. My back swore at me, but the bruises on my face defended me. They said that my back didn't have to go surfing, it could have objected, it should have said something. My buttocks agreed. I poured myself a beer and drank it slowly. I thought about loss; my father, my childhood, my surfboard, clean seas at every beach, Gershwin, killed by a brain tumour that should have been caught. I thought about gain; a decent can of beer, my mother, Estelle, an area of low pressure that was so close I could touch it.

Estelle came at half past ten, and made me lie on my stomach while she dabbed my back with antiseptic. I'd told her that I didn't need it, but she insisted. She told me that I could catch a nasty infection. Sennen is a Blue Flag Beach, though macerated sewage is discharged one hundred and thirty metres from the sea wall. Then she told me that I was an idiot to go out in a storm, but I told her that what I did was my own business, and to shut it. She smacked my arse for that, and I yelped in pain. 'Serves you right,' she said, 'you deserve more.'

'More?' I said. 'And what about you? What have you done to deserve more?'

'What haven't I done?'

'I don't know. You tell me.' I sat up and held her chin in my hand. It was soft and when it caught the light, you could see hundreds of minute blonde hairs on it. 'Why do you work here?'

'They're my parents. When I left school, they gave me the job.'

'That was nice of them . . .'

'Beggars can't be choosers,' she said.

'Are you a beggar?'

'I'd be out of here in a flash, but do you want to know how difficult it is to get work round here?'

'Is that a question?'

'Yes.'

'It's difficult everywhere,' I said.

She nodded, wiped some antiseptic cream off her fingers and said, 'I got English and Biology, Design and Technology; didn't do me any good.'

'You've got them?'

'Yeah. And History.'

'And you left school?'

'And Geography,' she said.

'Geography?'

'Yeah.'

'You like Geography?'

'Hate it.'

'Oh,' I said.

'Why?'

'I'm doing Geography at university.'

'You're at university?' She put her hand to her mouth and laughed. 'You?'

'Yeah. Start next week, at Exeter.'

'You're kidding.'

'What do you mean?'

She looked deeply into my eyes, as if searching for a lie, then shook her head and said, 'Nothing.'

'Yeah,' I said, 'a whole lot of nothing,' and I grabbed her around the waist. She yelped, wriggled away and ran to the window, opened it and stood on the balcony. She was really beautiful; you should have seen her there. I got up from the bed and joined her, and we looked at the night together. The drizzle had passed and the clouds were beginning to thin. A single star shone through, and a glimmer of the moon. The Pendeen light swept its regular beam across the sea, glittering the waves. I saw the swell and I sensed it building, the feeling came to me and then it went, then it came again and went again, the sea in me and the smell in the air. Estelle planted kisses on my shoulder and I pinched her waist. 'Given the choice,' she said, 'wouldn't you like to live here?'

'Oh yeah,' I said, 'it's magic.'

'If there was anything else going, I'd be out of here in a shot, but I'd have to come back. You can leave the place but the place never leaves you.'

'I know what you mean.'

She laid her hand on my back. 'When I was a kid, I wanted to be a nurse. Barry used to be my patient, and on a good day he'd let me perform operations on him.'

'Barry?'

'My brother. He's in the navy now; he was a useless patient, but I was a brilliant nurse.'

'I bet you were.'

'You think so?'

'I never say what I don't mean. I bet you were and I bet you could be. You're wasted here.'

'Not wasted,' she said, 'bored maybe. Irritated sometimes, too . . .'

'By me?'

'Not by you,' she said, 'never by you. You're weird, but that makes a change. This place can be like God's waiting room; Mum and Dad like to run a tight ship. You're the youngest guest we've had for months.' She pointed down to the car park. The Beetle was dwarfed by a Jaguar, a Mercedes and a pair of Volvos. 'I think they'd like you to park round the back.'

'Would they?'

'But they'll be impressed when I tell them you're going to university.'

'Maybe I'm lying.'

'Are you?'

'No,' I said, 'but I'm cold.'

We went back inside, closed the windows, poured some wine, dimmed the light and lay on the bed. Standing outside hadn't cooled Estelle's body, which was hot. Hot as a smoking gun or the fat barrels of Supertubes. She said, 'Do I surprise you?'

'Why should you do that?'

'The first time I saw you I thought yeah; I'll eat him alive.'

'I'm waiting.'

She took a mouthful of wine, swilled it around before swallowing, and leaned towards me. 'Anytime, slim.'

My body dipped and then drowned its aches and bruises in her. As soon as we stopped talking and slipped our arms around each other, I felt as though June was taking November and strangling it, that all the hot weather in the world was being bottled and sent to my head at wholesale prices. The bottle was glowing, I took its lid off and felt some of the heat escape. It clouded over us, and began to drip on our heads. We began to slobber each other's necks, she tugged at my trousers, I unbuttoned her blouse and eased it off her shoulders. The bra was unhooked, her skirt was around her ankles; she kicked it off and we watched it arc through the room to land on the television. 'Good goal,' I said, and she said, 'Oh God, you're not into football, are you?'

'Hate it,' I said. 'I hate all sports.'

'What's surfing?'

'Surfing's surfing.'

'Sure,' she laughed.

'Sport's for people in clichés with shorts on the brain.'

'Shouldn't that be the other way round?'

'Should it?' I said.

'My old man used to play tennis for England. He wore shorts.'

'What happened?'

Estelle shrugged. 'He says it was his back, but I heard he didn't have the bottle.'

'Oh dear,' I said.

'He can't help it,' she said. 'He tries his best . . .'

'. . . But his best wasn't good enough!' I said, as my shirt sailed across the room. 'Whoops,' I said.

'Whoops what?'

'Whoops I think I love you,' and I nestled into her breasts.

'Love now, is it?'

'You're not going to tell me not to fall in love with you, are you?' I said.

'Why would I say that?'

'It's something some women say.'

'Do they?'

'Yeah.'

'Daft fuckers,' she said.

'Yeah.'

'You can do anything you like with me,' she said, and she pushed me off her and crawled to the foot of the bed. She took the legs of my jeans and wrenched them off. As she did, she pulled me down the bed and rubbed my back down the sheet. I yelled.

She approached me backwards, moving on her hands and knees, wriggling over my legs, my stomach and then sat on my chest. 'I'm sorry,' she said, and grabbed my prick. It was pulsing like a nervous throat. If it could have sung, it would have. 'Is that better?' and she started to rub.

'Yeah,' I said, and I took her around the waist, pulled her towards me, parted her lips with my tongue, and began to suck.

The Communist Master of Disease could not have covered me more completely, its flesh never had the power that Estelle stored in her fleshy rolls. People say that the cathedral waves of Hawaii's Waimea Bay contain enough energy that, if harnessed, could light all the towns of the island's north shore. Waves of water, waves of salt and waves of flesh. She ground into my face. My eyes were open, it was dark, but all around me little folds of skin trilled against my mouth, and her hair whispered. There was a whistling and a singing, and a deep feeling in my head. Everything was full of fish and swimming in flesh, exactly like Portugal. It was sour and molten, raging and quiet, all these things at once and all these things again and again. The whistling was an old tune and it was a new tune, and there were sixteen different ways of singing it. Each way wore a different hat but the same shoes, and the shoes were polished with lust. Estelle leant forward and began to nip my stomach. After each nip she licked the spot, and kissed it; I reached forward, took her breasts in my hands and weighed them. I held her nipples between my forefingers and my index-fingers and squeezed. She sat down hard, I gasped and blew for air, she shifted down the bed and looked over her shoulder at me. I wiped my face, took some hairs out of my mouth and said, 'What a sunny day.'

'Bet your arse.'

I slapped hers.

She lifted one leg so she was kneeling beside me, flipped me over and smacked mine with both her hands. Tears shot into my eyes, I yelled into the pillow, turned over again and grabbed her wrists. 'Yeah,' we were saying, and I was in her, she was grinding over me, fast and faster, moving, heaving, our flesh going slap, slap, slap, slap, slap. I was completely covered by her, I was a hot-blooded singer, I was pigeons flying up and fluttering around, I was a Gregory Peck film I'd never seen but always promised to, and I was a barrel of maple syrup. I was every track The Waterboys recorded between December 1981 and July 1985, from 'December' through 'All the things she gave me' and 'Be my enemy' to 'This is the sea'. I was some rare piano improvisations that

Jack Gibbons transcribed from Gershwin's original piano rolls, too late for my Dad to hear. Two hands becoming six, six turning to twelve. I was not bitter at all, and I was exactly the right age to be doing the things I was doing. I cried that I loved her, and she wailed that she wanted me every night, and that she didn't want to leave that room, ever. We made extreme flopping and juiced noises, we raged and sweated, we laughed and laughed, and all my pain was gone. The bed was going like a thousand dogs barking and tapping spoons on metal trays, it was loud but the quieter sounds were noisier to our ears, the knock on the door, the rattling of a pane of glass in the window, the person in the next room smoking a last cigarette, then cleaning his teeth. She was tighter than ever or I was bigger than I have ever been, and her fleshy folds hung all around me like tiny curtains. Her eyes were open and huge, and her lips folded over her teeth, her tongue came out and wiggled. The person in the next room finished cleaning his teeth, and there was another knock on the door.

I began to seek and find Estelle's moles. She had them on many parts of her body. Cheek, neck, shoulders, a little clump on the rise of her right breast, and a hive of them under the left. I touched each one with the pointy tip of my tongue, and felt how they were raised from the surface of her skin. I listened to them but they made no sound. I heard the door knock again and found a mole on her stomach, just below her navel. It was in the shape of a tear, and bearded with downy brown hairs, and when I touched it, Estelle let out a long, loud moan, as if I had given her a clitoris. I took it between my thumb and finger and rolled it around, and I lowered my mouth. I thought I heard it squeak, I thought I was holding a mouse in the palm of my hand. I thought I could smell a rock-pool. Sea urchins. Whelks. Starfish. Limpets. The peeling varnish on an old wooden board, the rust on some car door and the taste of candy floss. Estelle's skin was as smooth as butter, glass, ice. Whoever was outside in the corridor thumped on the door, and now I said 'Your old man?' to Estelle.

She brushed her hair back, pulling it away from her forehead with a raised arm, stretching back above me. I planted a kiss in the middle of her stomach, she held her head in her arms and shrugged. 'I don't know,' she whispered, 'and don't know if I care.' She leant over and pulled the duvet off the floor and covered herself. I got up, wrapped a towel around my waist, opened the door a foot and poked my head out.

It was her old man. He had this huge expression on his face, all boiling oil, midnight confessions and the Communist Master of Disease. He opened his mouth, and I saw the words sitting inside it, waiting to jump out. 'What the hell's going on in here?'

I said, 'What the fuck's it to you?'

'We're trying to run a decent hotel here,' he said.

'It's pretty decent,' I said. 'The food's great, the view's wonderful and the room service is brilliant.'

'Room service?' he said, and he tried to see through the crack in the door.

'Yes.'

'But you haven't used room service.'

'I had some sandwiches the night before last. They were very good. Yeah.' I let my grip go on the door; he saw me relax and, before I had the chance to stop him, had barged past me and was in the room.

'Hi, Dad,' said Estelle.

Her old man's face was like a cartoon face; it began to turn purple from the chin up, his eyes bulged with fury and little puffs of steam blew from his nostrils. Her breasts were sitting in front of her and her hair was all over the place. One of her feet was sticking out of the duvet. She looked at it and wiggled her toes. He opened his mouth and tried to force something out, but it was trapped.

'What are you doing here?' she said.

'Yeah?' I said.

'It's late,' she said.

'Very,' I whispered.

For a moment he looked awkward, completely at sea while we sailed safely around him. I watched his hands. He made fists with them and then opened them, then fists again, open again, then fists again. His knuckles were white, he tried to take a step towards the bed, but his legs would not move. He opened his mouth and his lips started to quiver. I thought he was about to go down on his knees and cry. His eyes fluttered, the purple colour did not leave his face. He closed his mouth and opened it again, like a fish. He pointed at Estelle and hissed, 'Go to your room.'

'I'm happy here,' she said.

'Estelle!'

'What?'

'GO!' The word cracked like a shot, and his pointing finger shook. He took a step towards the bed, I stepped between him and her, he looked at me as if I wasn't there, and then he touched me.

'Hey!' I yelled, 'Don't you touch me!' I slapped his hand away. 'And get out of my room!'

'Your room?' He tried an ironic laugh, but it came out like a hiccup.

'Yeah!'

'You,' he said, and now he focused on me, 'get out of my way.' He pushed past me, I stumbled back and fell on to the bed. Estelle suddenly leapt over me, avoided her father's lunge, and shot out of the door. She ran naked down the corridor, I watched her go, heard a door open and slam shut, a lock turned, her father stared down at me, I glared back at him, he said, 'You're out of here in the morning.'

'I was leaving anyway.'

'You good-for-nothing . . .'

'Oh,' I said, 'so you have got some imagination,' and I laughed at him.

'What?'

'And someone told me about your second service.'

The purple began to drain from his face. I imagined it filling his shoes and staining his socks.

'What was it?' I said. This was better than using a fist. 'No balls?'

For a moment, as a pale, slack colour filled his cheeks, I thought he was going to hit me, but then he turned and left the room. I got off the bed and slammed the door at his back, and listened to his footsteps in the corridor. They were quick and heavy, and all his memories were in them like lead.

FIFTEEN

I woke early, wrote a note for Estelle and took it to her room. I pushed it under her door, then went to Mother's room. She was sitting at her dressing-table, brushing her hair. She smiled when she saw me, stood up and kissed me on the cheek. 'Duncan,' she said, 'I'm sorry about last night. I didn't mean to scare you.'

'We were worried. Clive was frantic.'

She hung her head and said in a dying voice, 'I'm nothing but trouble for you.'

'No you're not . . .'

'And for Clive. Isn't what I said about him true?'

'Yeah,' I said. 'He's a good bloke. I like him.'

She smiled, turned and went back to the dressing-table. She put her hairbrush down, and took a towel to the bathroom. While she was in there, I said 'I've got to move out.'

'Sorry, dear?' she called.

'There was a bit of trouble last night.'

'What sort of trouble?' She came out of the bathroom carrying her dressing-gown.

'Estelle was in my room . . .'

She hung the gown on the back of the door. 'Not the manager's daughter?'

'Yeah.'

'She's a nice girl . . .'

'He came to the room,' I said, 'knocked on the door; we were in bed together.'

'And why did he do that?'

'To complain about the noise.'

Mother looked sideways at me, then put her hand up to my face and tapped my cheek with the tips of her fingers. 'The noise?'

'Yeah.'

She shook her head, went to the windows and opened them. She stepped on to the balcony. I followed her, and we looked down at the cliff path, the rocks and sea. The swell was running strong, the sky was blue and the sun was shining. There were some puffs of cloud, but they moved high and fast. A pair of seagulls flew by, flapping their wings with long, lazy beats. They turned to look at us, the one in front squawked and shat on my car. The air was fresh and bright, like a lemon.

I could smell a wave, far out to sea. As I stood there, it was only a hump, cruising at twenty-five knots in open ocean under a bowling sky. It was strung out in an irregular line and, though it had sensed land, it had not slowed. It was six hours away. I looked at my watch, shook it and held it to my ear. It was half past seven. Mother said, 'And so you've got to leave?'

'Yeah.'

'Where are you going?'

'Porthleven. There's a bed and breakfast I know. Mrs Kertész's. She'll give me a room. I'll leave you her address.'

'Have you paid your bill?'

'Not yet.'

'Let me.'

'No.'

'I insist,' she said. 'Absolutely.'

'But . . .'

'Tell them to put it on mine.' She looked straight in my eyes and did not let go. 'If it's the last thing I do . . .'

'OK,' I said.

'Good.'

'But let's meet later. On the harbour wall.'

'Where?'

'Porthleven.' I took her hand and squeezed it. 'You know how to get there?'

'I'll find it,' she said.

'Six o'clock tonight. I want to talk to you properly.'

'What about?'

'Last night,' I said, 'when you said that you knew what you had to do. What was that?'

She turned away. 'What I thought then I don't know if I think now. Too much confusion and not enough time. Of course, that's my own fault . . .'

'Not really,' I said.

'Really.'

'Are you going to Canada?'

She stared ahead, and her gaze was caught by another seagull. She followed its flight, over the scrubby tops of the cliffs, down towards the hotel, past the balcony and round the back. 'It's Saturday,' she said, 'and Canada's Monday. Monday's another day.' She walked back into the room, dabbed her neck with perfume, looked at the bottle and said, 'Always put it on cold skin. The skin's more important than the scent. Did you know that?'

'No.'

'Well now you do,' she said.

She went to breakfast and I went to Clive's room. He was brushing his teeth; as he gargled, I told him I was leaving, and asked him to make sure Mother visited me in Porthleven. He spat, wiped his mouth and said, Why? Don't you trust her?'

'I trust her,' I said, 'but I don't think she trusts herself.'

'What do you mean by that?'

'I think that half of her doesn't know what the other half's doing, and that the ignorant half will get the better of her.'

'Well,' he said, unrolling his shirt-sleeves and buttoning them up, 'if that happens, there's precious little we can do about it.'

'Aren't you worried?'

He took his jacket from the back of a chair and slipped it on. 'Of course I am, but worrying's not going to help her.'

'What is?'

'Acting normally,' he said. 'That's the only thing you can do; if you start trying to protect her from something you imagine she's going to do, you'll only end up pushing her in that direction.'

'And what direction's that?'

'The one you're thinking about . . .'

'You don't think she needs protection?'

'Absolutely not.' He went to the window and closed it. 'Believe me,' he said.

'That's difficult.'

He patted my shoulder. 'I know what you went through,' he said, 'and I know exactly what you're afraid of, but the best thing you can do is act normally.'

'These aren't normal circumstances.'

'No,' he said, 'but do you want them to be?'

'I wouldn't mind.'

'You surprise me.'

'Why?'

'Aren't you the sort of lad who thrives on the unusual?'

'Yeah,' I said, 'but there's unusual and there's unusual.'

'Let's not split hairs.'

'That's not what I'm doing. All I want is . . .' I looked away from him, through the window.

'Breakfast?'

'I'm not hungry.'

'Well, I am,' and with another pat on my shoulder he said, 'don't worry. She'll be alright.'

'Is that a promise?'

'No, but I'm a doctor. I'm not used to making promises.'

I laughed.

'But at least I can make you laugh.'

'That's not because you're funny.'

'Why then?'

'I laugh because I don't want to cry.'

'There's nothing wrong with crying.'

'I know,' I said, 'but there's something wrong when you can't.'

He kept his hand on my shoulder for another moment, then took it away, ran his hand through his hair and opened the bedroom door. 'Come on,' he said, 'it's another day.'

'Saturday,' I said.

'Yes,' he said, 'and I love Saturdays.'

I carried my bags down to the reception and rang the bell on the desk. After a minute, Estelle's father appeared from his office. I stared straight at him, he glared back, the air between us was like steam off a vindaloo. His eyes had very small pupils, and his cheeks were covered in a network of fine lines. I said, 'My mother's going to settle the bill.'

'Which bill?' he said.

'Three nights half-board and a plate of sandwiches from room service.'

'Oh,' he said, 'that bill.'

'Sorry,' I said, 'but are you trying to be funny?'

'No.'

'Now,' I said, 'that *is* funny.'

'You,' he said thinly, 'will be laughing on the other side of your face.'

'Is that a threat?'

'It's a promise,' he said smartly.

'Oh,' I said, 'I think I'm going to shit myself. In fact, I think I'm going to now.'

He reached out a hand, I took a step back. 'I'm going to have you,' he said.

'Unfortunate choice of words,' I said.

He looked quizzical. He turned what he'd said over in his mind, looked at the words, took them apart, put them back together and then shook his head. 'And you're unfortunate,' he said.

'Ouch!' I said. 'I'm going to tell my Dad about you.'

'Go on then.'

'No,' I said, '*that* was a joke. My Dad's dead.'

He narrowed his eyes, thinking about this. As he thought, I picked up my bag and left the River Cove Hotel. I took a deep breath of air at the top of the steps, and listened to my wave. It was closer, still cruising, and everything was beautiful. I ran down the steps, jumped into the Beetle and it started first time. It always does, it never fails, and I drove away. Estelle was waiting for me around the corner. As I approached her, she put out her thumb and a big smile covered her face. I stopped, she threw her bag in the back and climbed in. She threw her arms around my neck and kissed it. I kissed hers, held her breasts through her shirt, put my nose in her hair, counted to twenty-five and then back again.

'You needn't have left the note,' she said. 'I was going to be here anyway.'

'Just checking,' I said.

'What a man.'

'What a woman.'

The road was dry and clear, and I drove with my elbow resting on the window ledge, The Waterboys singing 'Somebody Might Wave Back', the wheel in one hand and Estelle's thigh under the other. The engine sounded as sweet as a nut, the gear-stick slipped easily between the gears, the sun was slowly rising. The sea shone like chrome and birds sang in the hedges. An aeroplane's vapour trail hung high above us, and the smell of salt and hot breath filled the car. I said, 'Did you see your old man?'

'No. I left by the back door. I saw Mum, said goodbye to her and the cat.'

'What did she say?'

'Miaow.'

'No, idiot.'

'Calling me an idiot?'

'Yeah, idiot.'

She reached across and tapped my cheek.

'Your Mum . . .' I said

'Nothing much. She's been expecting it. I think she'd do the same, given half the chance.'

'Why doesn't she?'

'She's scared, I suppose. She wouldn't know what to do, and I don't think she knows what he would do. The stupid thing is, he's all hot air. He threatens and makes a show of it, but when the shit hits the fan, he's the first to take cover.'

'Typical Tory wanker?'

'I don't know about the typical, but yeah. You know, a few years ago, when the stock market crashed, he lost thousands. Now he's being skinned alive by business rates, he gets half the number of guests he got last year, VAT's got him by the bollocks and he still votes for them.'

I laughed like a drain.

'If the papers told him to stick his head in a bucket of

shit and wait two years for eighteen fat camels to pass by in a snowstorm, he'd do it.' She shook her head. 'Poor bastard.'

I slowed down to let a farmer drive some cows across the road, and I didn't stop laughing. 'I'm sorry,' I said.

'No you're not,' she said.

I waved at the farmer and he waved back with his stick. His cows were big and healthy, and started running and bucking when they got in their field. There were big rocks in the field, sticking out of the grass like the backs of dead elephants, and we passed a barn with holes in its roof that had been patched with straw and cow shit. We followed a milk tanker for a few miles, and stopped for breakfast outside Penzance, at a café on the main road. We drank tea from mugs the size of buckets, and ate toast cut as thick as a brick. The marmalade was sad and thin, and cheap margarine came between the two, running over the crusts of the bread and pooling on the plate, but it didn't spoil the occasion. This was a feast. I said, 'I've got to get a board today.'

'Where?'

'I know someone in Porthleven. He'll set me up.'

'And then what?'

'I'm surfing. There's a big wave coming and it's got my name written on it.'

'Like a bullet?'

'No,' I said, 'yesterday's was like a bullet. Today's is the Master of the Cure.'

'What?'

'The Master of the Cure.' I filled my mouth with toast and marmalade, chewed slowly and pointed out of the window. Over the road, past the heliport and a warehouse, St Michael's Mount rose out of the sea. The sun glinted off the Abbey's windows. 'It's there . . .' I said, swallowing, 'two hours away.' I banged my chest. 'I can feel it; I know it, and when that happens, look out!'

She grabbed my hand, pulled it towards her and rubbed it in her lap. 'Look out for what, Dunc?'

'Just look out,' I said.

She squeezed my hand. 'And when I've done that?'

'I'm all yours. Do what you want with me.'

'I was going to do that anyway.'

I finished my toast, licked around my teeth and swilled my mouth with tea. 'Good,' I said.

'Is that all you can say?'

'What more can I say? My mother's going to Canada on Monday, at least that's what she says she's doing. Then I've got to go back to Sussex, pick up my stuff and head this way again. This time next week I'll be in Exeter.'

'You've got a place to live?'

'Yeah.'

She rubbished her hair and drank some tea. 'I like Exeter,' she said. 'There're some good shops there.'

'You can come if you want.'

'Yeah?'

'Of course,' I said. 'No problem.'

She sat back and ran her finger around the rim of her mug. The sun shone through the café's windows and splattered across the floor in stripes and ovals. Steam billowed out of the kitchen door, and the sound of sizzling bacon crackled through the air. The cook came over and took our empty plates. 'Anything else for you?' he said. He was a fat, bald man with a speck of egg yolk on his forehead. 'More tea?'

I shook my head and Estelle said, 'No thanks.'

He looked at her and licked his lips. He had a tattoo on his arm in the shape of a heart, with 'MUM' scrolled underneath it, and he had the word 'LUST' written across his eyes. His nose was flat, a boxer's nose. His eyes burned and flashed, they looked up and down Estelle, his breathing was difficult and heavy. 'Sure?' he wheezed.

'Yeah,' I said, 'we're sure . . .'

He didn't look at me.

' . . . Thanks,' I said.

Estelle looked at me. 'OK?' she said.

'Ready when you are.'

At ten o'clock, the wave began to feel the seabed in its feet and it began to slow. It narrowed its watery eyes and focused on the Cornish shore, and the Cornish shore focused on it. It began to throw spindrift from its lip, and it filled its cheeks as it moved. The sound it made came from its solid and roaring throat, crescendoing steadily, its heartbeat was slow and regular, and all the fish that swam through it moved carefully. I stopped the car above Porthleven, shaded my eyes and looked out to sea, but I couldn't see it. Estelle put her hand on my knee; I looked at it. She was wearing a short brown skirt, and had bare legs. Her knees were like pink oranges, her eyebrows were pencil thin and her lips pouted. I kissed her. 'Estelle,' I said.

'Yes?'

'I meant what I said.'

'What was that?'

'About Exeter. Come with me,' I said. 'I want you to. I'm all set up there; all you'd have to do is move in.'

'Sure about that?'

'Yeah. You're everything I want.'

'Everything?' she whispered.

I looked at the sea and I looked at Porthleven. I saw gulls over houses and the sun on roofs. I saw people coming and going from the houses, and cars in the streets. I saw a dog trotting along the pavement, and an old woman in her garden. She was pruning a bush, she was putting the cuttings in a basket. There was a line of washing flapping behind her. I watched a couple walking along the beach, hand in hand. 'Everything,' I said.

SIXTEEN

We stayed with Mrs Kertész, a big Hungarian widow with a voice like fog-horn. When she answered the door, she cried 'Duncan!' and threw her arms around me. For a moment, everything went dark as she squeezed me, and my head disappeared into her enormous bosom. She smelt of cabbage and beef, and I wheezed. She cried 'Duncan!' again. 'Let me look at you!'

She stood back, her arms spread, breathing heavily. 'You look so well!' she boomed, and when she looked at Estelle, she said, 'And you've brought me a girl!'

'Hi,' said Estelle, holding her hand out.

'Come in,' said Mrs Kertész, shaking it. 'You're welcome to my home.'

We sat in the kitchen and drank black tea. Mrs Kertész didn't keep milk in the house. 'Any animal that needs more than one stomach must have something wrong with it,' is one of her favourites. Another is 'More beetroot?' Her face is the colour of beetroot, and she wears her hair piled up on top of her head, kept in place with a dozen clips. She gave us a room at the top of the house, with a window that opened on to a spreading view of the sea, and understood when I said that there was a wave coming, and that I had to buy a board. She made me promise to give her all my news later, and when I said, 'I'll try,' she slapped the top of my head and told me that I'd do more than that. She turned to Estelle, said, 'This is a boy that needs watching,' and let rip with a barrage of laughs that snapped, wheezed and popped like balloons all around us.

'You're telling me,' said Estelle.

'You never know what his sort are up to, do you?'

'Don't worry. I keep my eye on him.'

'And I think you keep more than that on him, no?'

'Maybe,' said Estelle.

'Just maybe?'

'Maybe more than that . . .'

'Good,' said Mrs Kertész, and she took Estelle's hand, patted it, turned it over and stroked the palm, as if she was preparing to read it. 'I can see we are going to be very good friends.' She looked at me and nodded. 'There is nothing like being very good friends, no?'

'No,' I said.

'Friends and lovers; they make the world go round. Where would we be without them?'

'I don't know.'

'I do,' she said, 'we'd be in the cow.'

'In the cow?'

'Oh yes. Deep in it, I think, and there'd be no way out.'

Estelle looked at me, and for a moment I thought her face was going to explode. Her cheeks were puffing and her eyes bulged. Little lines appeared at the corners of her mouth, and she snorted another ballooning laugh.

'Oh yes,' said Mrs Kertész, 'and that's another thing, laughter. Did you know, when you laugh, you make drugs in your brain?'

'Do you?'

'You do, absolutely. That's why you feel good when you do it,' and she laughed too. 'I want everybody laughing in my house, and then I'm feeling happy.'

I laughed.

'See?' said Mrs Kertész. 'Whatever your unhappiness, you are feeling better already.'

'I feel better just for seeing you,' I said.

She ruffled my hair. 'Nice boy,' she said, and when she'd finished, I tidied my hair. 'And now you must catch your wave.'

'Yeah?'

'And it's called?' she said.

'The Master of the Cure.'

'Really!' said Mrs Kertész, and she turned to Estelle. 'Doesn't he think up the strangest names?'

'You're telling me.'

'It's an antidote to the Communist Master of Disease.'

'Argh . . .' she went, and her face lost its joy. Mrs Kertész had escaped from Communists in 1950.

'Sorry,' I said.

'Why can't you call your waves nice things?'

'I don't know . . .'

'You could have called it "Estelle",' she said.

'Maybe,' I said.

'Maybe?' said Mrs Kertész. She laughed now, and said to Estelle, 'What do you think of maybe?'

'Not much,' she said.

'Is he a silly boy or not?'

'I don't know,' said Estelle, and she took my arm.

'Love never does, does it?' said Mrs Kertész.

'No.'

It was time I bought a long board, a Malibu, and time I changed my style. Enough rip and slash, enough speed on the waves, enough cutting up in the swell. I went to Laughin' Bob's Shack, on the front. Bob's a bald man, I've never seen him wearing anything but board-shorts, a T-shirt and Tiki Walkabout Slaps. He was born in Birmingham, but moved to Cornwall when he was six. He used to surf, but stopped when he wiped out at Thurso and smashed his knees on the reef.

Now one leg is shorter than the other, the scars are florid, his balance is gone, and his nerve with it. Now he satisfies himself by shaping boards, fixing dings, watching breaks from beaches, and drinking beer. When I called on him, he was in his workshop, working in a cloud of fibreglass, the noise of his sanders and cutters filling the air. I yelled 'Bob!' and he didn't look up. 'Bob! BOB!'

I didn't want to surprise him, I didn't want to make him jump and lose grip of his sander, so I stood to one side and waited. There were posters on the walls: Tom Curren at Hossegor, a couple of guys paddling out from Bell Beach, Victoria. A topless woman in a Fistral slot. A wall of water breaking along Hawaii's north shore, a circle of Sex Wax stickers. A flying boat landing in a tropical lagoon, a solitary surfer standing with his back to a setting sun. Dying surf cruising towards a sandy shore. Bob looked up and saw me; he stopped working, flicked a switch off and yelled, 'Duncan!'

'Bob!'

'Long time no see!' He roared with laughter, wiped his hands on a damp cloth and we shook. 'What're you doing?'

'The usual,' I said. 'Waiting for the big one.'

He laughed again, looked at Estelle, looked back at me, smiled and mouthed, 'Yeah?'

'Fuck off,' I mouthed.

'Sure,' he said .

'But I need a board.'

'Wonders will never cease? What happened?'

'I got wiped out at Sennen. I lost my Tuna.'

'How many times have I told you?' he said. 'Use a leash.'

'Very funny,' I said.

He slapped my back and we went through to the shop.

The boards stood in soldiered rows, all fresh, all potential, all shiny and new. I told him that I was moving on, that I was ready for a new day. 'I want a Malibu.'

'Mod or trad?'

'Trad.'

'OK,' he said, and he clicked his fingers. 'This is the one you want,' and he picked out a big blue one. 'Nine Six. It's a pistol.' He stroked its deck, tapped its nose and rubbed its decal with the palm of his hand. 'You'll love it.'

I held it.

'What d'you think?'

'It's beautiful,' I said. 'I think I could live with it.'

'And a beautiful price too.'

'I bet.'

'To you . . .'

'To me?'

'Yeah. Seeing as you're the worst customer I ever had . . .'

'How much?'

He told me.

Fuck.

'Size-to-weight ratio's as good as it gets,' he said. 'You won't find better.'

'I'm sure,' I said.

'Why do I believe you?'

'Because I know as much about it as you do?'

Bob looked at Estelle. 'Does he?' he said.

'Don't ask me,' she said.

'Oh yeah,' I said, 'Bob, this is Estelle. Estelle, Bob.'

'How you doing?'

'OK.'

'She wants a T-shirt,' I said.

'Do I?' she said.

'Yeah,' said Bob, and leaving me holding the board, he took her to a rack at the front of the shop. 'There you go,' he said. 'Boardwalk, Billabong, Stussy, Life's a Beach, Sex Wax. If they make it, we've got it.'

'And if they haven't,' I said, 'it's not worth buying. That right, Bob?'

'Bet your arse, Dunc.'

'No,' I said, 'I never bet that.'

'That's not what I heard,' said Bob.

'What you heard's an echo,' I said.

'Do you ever think Dunc doesn't know what he's on about?' Bob said to Estelle.

'Never,' she said.

'Ha!' I said.

'Yeah,' said Bob, 'and ha! to you, little boy.'

'Sure.'

'I think you're too good for him,' he said to her.

'Dream on,' I said.

Estelle wore her Sex Wax T-shirt, and I carried my Nine Six Malibu to the beach. The sun was high, clouds flew and the Master of the Cure was close. We kissed at the high-tide line, she ran her fingernails down my spine and then I waded into the water. It was blue and cold, and though there were other surfers there, I felt alone. I stared ahead, I did not flinch. I put my ear to the sea and heard my wave coming; it was whispering at me, instructing me. I splashed my face and chest, pushed the board ahead, lay down and began to paddle out.

The swell was big and powerful, and it roared from its lips to its feet, thrusting up and pushing down, round and round and round. At that moment I was two minutes from a place I was born to see, I was the tip of a waiting bullet, and the edge of a steady knife. The pains in my back and my arse were gone, and all the worries in my head were drifting above me like pigeons. In a lull between sets, I stopped paddling and listened to the current as it dragged shingle and rocks along the seabed. It rustled and twitched, and all the tiny creatures that lived in it moved slowly. There was peace in motion, motion in the silence and all the silence spoke. A wave broke in front of me; I rolled under it, paddled through and up again, into another lull, then another, and then another, the last.

The Master of the Cure was building in front of me, it was a living wave, as fleshy as I could wish. I turned to the right and felt the power that thrust ahead of it. This came as an electric pulse through the water; I counted to ten, the swell filled and pushed, the seconds lengthened, I caught each one in the palm of my hand, turned them over, inspected them, rubbed them against my cheek and then I stood up.

You know that feeling when you're asleep and dreaming but you're about to wake up. The dream exists in some half-place, its pictures and the feeling it gives you fills your body, and though you know it's not happening to your conscious self, you think it could be. You're about to be killed, you're falling miles, you can see the ground coming up to meet you and feel the wind rushing through your hair. You're facing a pack of wild dogs. You've been told that you have to walk a thousand miles through fire, you're in a room full of naked women, and every one of them has your name tattooed on her forehead. You're walking through the carriages of a speeding train, and though the other passengers are staring at you, you think you're alright. Then you look down and you realise that you forgot to get dressed that morning. You look up and see your clothes in the luggage rack, and though they're within easy reach, you can't get them. You open your eyes a little and know it's a dream, but is it? When you close them, the dream images are projected on to the backs of your eyes, you can smell the worry and taste the horror. You try to force yourself awake but nothing works, you're glued to your bed and your feet refuse to work. Your brain does not obey your wishes, it holds on and will not let go. Time becomes a single, long second; as I was picked up by the Master of the Cure, this is exactly what I felt. I was suspended between my hopes and reality, I hung like a kite between the sea and the sky. My new board was light and fresh, my feet held it like a clamp and the sound of the wave seemed to come from miles away. I cried out, and my cry broke from my mouth with pain though I felt no pain, only joy. The wave was breaking in a perfect line, I slowed to let it catch up with me and then it started to barrel behind me. I looked over my shoulder and watched it approach, as clean as a new sheet and absolutely round. I crouched, straightened and it came to me.

I saw Estelle in it, her hair, her thighs and her breasts, her nipples lowering towards me, and I saw my mother's fading face reflected there, in a tube so long and dry and perfect that it appeared to stretch back miles. As I surfed it, not a single drop of water touched my back, though I was surrounded by the stuff. The shore had disappeared, the sky did not exist, and the reef was under my complete control. All I could see was foam above me and a curl of spray ahead. I shifted my weight to the tail of the board, I slowed and dipped, reached out and touched the walls of the tube. I could write on the sea, and the sea held the letters. I shouted and my words echoed, and they grabbed the sound of my wake and kissed it. I kissed myself and I kissed the wave, the wave held me and would not let go. It told me that it had waited for me, that it belonged to me, and that I could do what I wanted with it. I could put it in a bag and take it on holiday with me, I could teach it Cantonese or how to tango. I leaned forward and looked out; there was a gull in the sky, and it screeched as it glided over me. This was a jealous screech, caught and then swallowed by the waves. I strained my head to watch, I hopped to the middle of the board, the tube began to weaken and shoot; I dropped out of it, went for a bottom turn, reversed and headed back the way I had come. I flipped off the white water that was breaking behind me and, as the wave began to fail, I turned under a section, crept back and re-entered, slowly this time, ahead of the breaking lip, exposed to the shore and the sky, and anyone who had waited for me to come saw me now, as if I had just been born.

Estelle waved, and when she waved, I waved back. The sun reflected off the palm of her hand, and her hair blew in the breeze. I yelled her name but the word was snatched by the sea, pushed under and drowned. I saw her mouth open but I didn't hear what she shouted. Another surfer dropped in behind me; a kid in a black suit riding a yellow board. He ripped and slashed behind me, I pushed ahead and let my weight kill the ride. I sank into the lump the Master of the Cure had become, and when I surfaced I watched its back cruising to the shore. I was alone at sea, and all the gifts I had ever wished for were filling my head. I flipped my board around and paddled out again, over the rising sets and on to another wave.

SEVENTEEN

I met my mother alone on the harbour wall. There were some fishermen there, and the smell of wood-smoke and weed in the air. The sky was clear and chill. We walked to the end of the pier, stood together and stared. Mother wore a thick overcoat. She took my arm and I felt her body shiver against me. There was an awful inevitability in her touch, a cold, pale and final thing, like a bone on ice. The swell was still running, waves were still breaking, and gulls were soaring and drifting over the sea. She sighed and said, 'Did you have a good day?'

'Yeah.' I said, 'brilliant. It was perfect; as good as it's ever been. And you?'

'Quiet,' she said. 'There was a very odd atmosphere at the hotel, but I don't suppose that surprises you?' Her voice rose and fell with the sea.

'No . . .'

'So we spent the day on the cliffs. We walked miles.'

'Nice?'

'It was beautiful.'

'And how's Estelle's old man?'

'I saw him this afternoon. He didn't look too happy.'

'Oh dear,' I said.

'Why do I think you don't mean that?'

'Because I don't.'

She shook her head at me, I laughed, and then we stood in silence for a minute and watched the sea beat against the foot of the harbour wall. It slapped and foamed and uncurled in a bubbling line from one end to the other. I coughed and said, 'So . . .'

'So?'

'Yesterday,' I said, 'in the cave . . .'

'Yes?'

'You said you knew what you were going to do.'

'Oh dear . . .'

'You did . . .'

'And you want to know?'

'Yeah,' I said. 'I don't want to be left in the lurch again. I want to know where you'll be.'

'Don't worry,' she said, 'you will.'

'But where's that going to be? Canada?'

She looked away. 'Canada . . .'

'You were so sure . . .'

'Yes.' Her voice turned hard. 'But I'm not now. Can you understand that?'

'Yeah,' I said, 'of course I can. I'm not hassling, but . . .'

'Hassling's exactly what you're doing.'

'Don't you think I'm entitled to?'

'No,' she said, 'but you obviously do.'

'I don't want to.'

'But you do it anyway.'

'Mother,' I said, 'I'm tired of all this.'

'All what?'

'This beating around the fucking bush.'

'Duncan! Please!'

'What?'

'That word,' she said.

'What word?'

'You know what I mean.'

'And it's what I mean.'

'I'm sure it's not.

'Just tell me!'

'Look,' she said, and she raised her voice. 'How can I?'

'But you said you knew!' The words cracked in my throat; I grabbed them before they fell, put them on some shelf in my head and said, 'You told both of us.'

'I did,' she said, and the voice was quiet again, 'but that was last night. All I think I know is that I'm not ready.'

'Not ready for what?'

'Either of you.'

'Why do you have to be ready? It's not a prerequisite for anything. In fact,' I said, 'I think it's better if you're not.'

'Why do you think that?'

'Because then it can only get better.'

'It takes two to tango, Duncan . . .'

'What's dancing got to do with it?'

'. . . But if one's got a bad foot, even if she wants to dance, she can't.'

'She can try.'

'Oh yes, she can try, but if she knows she's only going to make it worse if she does, then what's the point?'

'Maybe her partner would appreciate the effort.'

'Maybe,' said my mother, 'but maybe not.' She looked straight into my eyes for a moment, then looked away, out to sea. The sun was slipping, and the sky was striped with pink and red, like a scar. Each stripe bled the dark that hid behind the light, and each beat of my heart echoed in my chest. I shivered, Mother shivered, and she sighed again.

'You won't . . .' I started, but failed.

'I won't what?'

'Nothing.'

'No!' she snapped, 'What?'

'Really. Nothing.'

'Duncan! What were you going to say?'

'Please, Mum.'

'Mum again, is it?'

'Yes,' I said.

'Tell me.'

'I can't.'

'Why not?'

'It's difficult.'

'I'm sure it is,' she said.

'Don't you think it is?'

'I wouldn't like to say.'

'You're not . . .' I failed again.

'I'm not what?'

'You're not going . . .' my thoughts stumbled, and the words tripped out after them, '. . . to Clapham Junction again, are you?'

'Ah,' she said, and now she put her arm around my shoulder. 'Clapham Junction . . .'

'Yes, Mother. Clapham Junction.'

'And it's back to Mother again . . .'

'Mum . . .'

'No, I don't think so,' she said, and she forced a smile. 'It's not a particularly nice spot.'

'You know what I mean!'

'And I think you know what I mean.'

'A straight answer?'

'No,' she said.

'That's it?'

'Yes.'

I ached, but there was nothing I could do about it. I wanted to know exactly what she was going to do, but I didn't want to go round in circles again. Straight lines are the thing, circles are useless. 'I meant what I said about Exeter,' I said. 'You could come and live with me. I've got a place sorted; I'd love it.'

'And I'd love it too,' she said, 'but I have to know I could cope with it. I've still got this sadness in me, this madness, and while I've got it, I don't trust myself. And if I don't trust myself, how can I expect anyone else to?'

'Excuses,' I said. 'You don't have to expect anything, just believe that other people trust you.'

She laughed. 'Do you?'

'I think so.'

'I think so's not enough.' She reached out her bony fingers and held my hand. 'If you want your mother to live with you, you've got to know so.'

'Why can't we just take a chance?'

'You might be able to do that, but I can't. I have to have my life mapped out, if I don't, I go to pieces. It happened once before, it could happen again. Give me time, Duncan, and I promise I'll be your mother again.'

'You never stopped being that.'

'Maybe not in name, but in every other way. I can't expect you to forgive me . . .'

I didn't argue with that, but when she took her hand from mine I grabbed it back, held tight and would not let go. 'I don't want to lose you again,' I said.

She said, 'You're not going to,' but her voice cracked, and all its edges fell apart.

'I am. I know it. Tonight, tomorrow morning, whenever; you're going to go away again and not come back.' I squeezed her hand, and she winced. 'Aren't you?'

She shook her head.

'Aren't you?' I raised my voice.

She looked away. I took her chin and turned her face towards me. 'Mother?'

'No,' she whispered.

'I don't believe you.' Her skin was cold, and I could feel her wrinkles quivering in my palms. Tears began to fill her eyes and they ran into the cracks between my fingers.

'I might go away,' she croaked, 'but I'll be back.'

'Will you?'

'How could I stay away?'

'You've done it once before . . .'

'Don't be cruel . . .'

'. . . You could do it again.'

'. . . I can't. I couldn't. You're my son, you're the image of your father, you're the only one I've got.'

'What about Clive?'

'Clive's too good for me.' She sniffed, deeply. She sounded like a broken engine. 'I don't want to hold him back.'

'Don't give me that self-pity. It doesn't suit you.'

'It's not self-pity, it's the truth.'

'Like hell it is!'

Now she twisted her head away from my hands, rummaged for a tissue, dabbed her eyes and blew her nose. She took a couple of heaving breaths and said, 'All this because of that.'

'What?'

'Your Dad didn't have to die . . .'

'But he did,' I said, 'and it's time you knew it.'

'Is it?'

'Yeah.'

She sighed and said, 'I'm close, I suppose, very close,' and she gently patted my knee. 'And I promise. You'll be the first to know when I do.'

I tried to believe her, but it was hard. The sun had set, the sky was creased with slashes of orange and red, lonely sea-birds cried along the shore. Below us, the water looked black and dead as it slapped against the harbour wall. The breaking waves curled and roared across the reef, their lips shooting lines of foam from west to east. One died and another was born, all virgins running together. My mother's face glistened, her eyes were sunk in their sockets, and as she wept, she took laboured breaths, and her lips curled back. I held her again hugging her as tight as I could without doing damage. I felt as though I was walking on eggshells, carrying sacks of orphaned kittens in a snowstorm. The moon rose behind us, the smell of wood-smoke still hung over the town. 'You promise?' I said.

'As long as I live,' she whispered, and the five words lodged in me and never let go. I felt an awful touch in the air, a certainty that brushed my face and left a mark there. Fate was drifting around us, and though we both knew it, there were no more words we could ever say to each other, no more half-thoughts or double meanings. I knew what she wanted to say, and though she didn't, I nodded to her as if she had. There was nothing I could do, and nowhere I could take her. Nobody could take her anywhere, only she had the means and the ticket. It wasn't born of cowardice and it didn't stink of self-pity; necessity is what she thought. Born from pain and kept in agony. I let her hold my hand for as long as she wanted and I let her go without trying to hold her back. Everyone has this journey to make, and we make it alone.

I killed my knowledge in a bottle of wine, and then, as I surfed inside the drink, Estelle and I made love in the high bedroom of Mrs Kertész's house. We made the beast with two backs, and as her back arched and mine straightened, the light of the moon smashed through the window and fell upon our bodies. A flighty wind bashed against the glass, the sky flew with violence, we were shining, we were absorbed, we were moving fast, smashing off our lips, I struggled to forget, and I did. I held her around the waist, she gripped the headboard, the bedstead rattled and shook and the moon would not let go. It clung to us, washing us with a blue light that played on our skins, dived into our hearts and paddled around. Her flesh smelt of sugar and sweat, and when I leant forward and buried my nose in her hair, I breathed sand and air. I lost myself in her, I paced myself but my paces ran ahead and I gasped to catch up. I pushed and I pushed and she pushed back at me, and we pushed together and fell off the bed.

I was lying on my back and she was lying on her back, on me. I wrapped my arms around her, she pinched me, sat up on my chest and said, 'What do you want me to do?'

'Ask another stupid question.'

'Yeah?'

'Go on,' I said.

'What's the difference between a banana?'

'That's a question?'

'Yeah,' she said, and she started to eat me.

'Turkey, turkey!' I cried.

'Slurp, slurp.'

'Gobble . . .'

'Gobble . . .'

I held two handfuls of her flesh, lifted her up and pulled her down, moved her around, twisted and ground her down. All her waves flapped around me, and her wet dripped on to my face. I opened my mouth, sucked her into it and banged my head on the side of the bed. When I tried to sit up, she sat down and would not let go. She did not let go until she had finished with me, and refused to let me get up until I had done her. There was no escape but I did not want it; I wanted years of this, stretching over me like a wall of water, tumbling and speeding, flailing and toppling. I wanted rolls of flesh and curls of hair filling my mouth, and every wail Estelle could give me. I wanted a tongue as big as a Scotch pancake, and a grip as tight as a tight hat. Did we come or did we go, where was the sun and where was the sea? My nose was running and there were tears in my eyes, though I couldn't remember starting to cry. It was hot; we got off the floor, she lay on the bed and I fetched another bottle.

We sat up together with glasses resting on our stomachs, the moon framed in the window. The smell of cabbage and beef drifted up from the kitchen, and the wailing sound of a Hungarian folk song. I wiped my eyes and said, 'Are you going to go away and never come back?'

'No.' She poured some more wine. 'Why?'

I blew my nose. 'Nothing.'

'Tell me,' she said.

I stared at my glass, swilled the wine around and shook my head. 'My mother,' I whispered. 'She's going to, and there's nothing I can do about it.'

She cuddled up to me and said, 'I'm sorry.'

'You don't have to say that. It's not your fault. It's nobody's fault; not unless you count my Dad, but nobody's counting him.'

She traced the outline of my left ear and said, 'Do you want to tell me what happened?'

'When?'

'To your Dad. How he died . . .'

'Estelle,' I said, and I turned on to my side and looked into her big eyes, 'that's what I love about you.'

'What?'

'You cut the crap. It's straight to the heart . . .'

'There's no point frigging around the edge.'

'Too true,' I said.

'So?'

'So,' I said, and I took a big mouthful of wine, 'he worked in a meat factory. He was the manager. He was a good one too, he liked to get down on the shop floor, mix with the workers. Everyone said he was the best, that he really cared about the people there. Mother and I were one family, they were another.'

'Did that make you feel jealous?'

'Hey!' I said, 'what are you; a fucking psychiatrist?'

'No.'

'You want to hear this?'

'Yes . . .'

'Then just listen, OK?'

'Sorry.'

'It's alright,' I said, and I kissed her. 'But it's difficult, this.' I drank more wine, poured some more and said, 'There was trouble with a mincer. It kept jamming, and every time it did, half the factory had to stop work. If they didn't have enough meat to put in the pies, well . . .

'They'd had the repairmen in, but as soon as they left, it broke down again. So Dad went down to the shop floor, and tried to do it himself. Like I said; he was that sort of bloke.'

'Did you say that?'

'Maybe not those words, but I meant it. You know.'

'Sorry.'

'He wasn't a mechanic, he only had to look at a spanner and he'd bleed, but he was the type of bloke who always wanted to have a go. Nothing held him back . . .'

'That's where you get it from.'

'Maybe,' I said, and I flicked some fluff off the bed and stared at the ceiling. There was a water-mark there, shaped like Africa. 'So,' I said, 'there he was, up a ladder, poking around inside the mincer, trying to get it to work. Everyone was standing around, waiting to get back to work. There were these big grinders. I suppose when they'd jammed somebody had forgotten to turn the power off, so they were straining against each other, ready to start up as soon as whatever was blocking them was freed. I think to start with he was poking around with a stick or something, trying to force them apart, but when that didn't work, he leant into the thing and used his hands . . .'

'Oh God.'

'It was stupid of him, but that's what he did . . .' I blew my nose again. 'Dead stupid.'

'I don't want to hear the rest.'

'I'm not sure I want to tell you.'

'Don't, please.'

'I think you've got the message, and I think I did . . .' I poured some more wine in both our glasses. 'I haven't eaten a pork pie for over eight years.'

'I'm never going to eat one again.'

'Of course,' I said, 'the chances of finding a finger in the average . . .'

'Duncan!'

'Yeah,' I said, 'I know,' and I got up, walked to the window and looked out. 'Yeah.'

'I'm sorry.'

'It wasn't your fault.'

'No, but you know what I mean.'

As the moon crossed that night sky, it surfed through the clouds. The gulls that followed it glowed luminous, flying silent and fast. The harbour was lit silver and blue, and the lines of waves stretched in pale, disappearing lines. The tide was low, and the sand was flat and washed. A car passed slowly along the road beneath me, and its headlights caught the figure of a single woman walking along the beach. She had her hands in her pockets and wore a headscarf; she picked up a stone and tossed it into the sea. The splash rippled in the moonlight, the circles spread and spread, the headlights turned and the figure was plunged into the shadows. The shadows were fat and dangerous, and every one stretched from its source like a warning. I was tired of warnings, I was tired of talking, I was tired. I turned to look at Estelle and she was looking at me. 'Come back to bed,' she said, and as every one of my tears burnt my face, I did.

EIGHTEEN

In the morning, Mother phoned Mrs Kertész, and left a message. We were in bed; Mrs Kertész tapped on the door and said, 'Duncan? Hello?' When I opened up, she took a step back into the corridor and said, 'She told me not to wake you, but she wants you to know she's not going to Canada tomorrow.'

I yawned and rubbed my eyes. 'Is she at River Cove?' I said.

Mrs Kertész looked at her watch. It was half-past nine. 'No,' she said. 'She was on her way out when she phoned. She said you'll see her soon.'

'What about Clive?'

'Who?'

'Her boyfriend.'

'Your mother has a boyfriend?'

'Yeah.'

'Oh, that's nice,' said Mrs Kertész. 'I think I should have a boyfriend, maybe. I need some help around here.'

'Where is he?'

'I haven't met him yet.'

'No,' I said, 'where's Clive?'

'Oh. She didn't say . . .'

'Did she say where she was going?'

'No.'

No. Back to the old days. Disappear without trace. Leave no clues. Worry people. Be selfish. I thanked Mrs Kertész, closed the door and started to dress. Estelle sat up in bed and put her arms out to me. 'Come here,' she said.

'No,' I said, 'I can't.'

'Why not?'

'It's my mother. She's checked out of the River Cove, and I never said goodbye.'

'She's checked out?'

'Yeah.'

'Do you want me to come?'

'No,' I said, 'you keep Mrs Kertész company.'

She held her breasts, pushed them towards me and said, 'I'd rather keep you company.'

I pulled on my trousers and went to her. 'I'll keep you company, Estelle,' I said, and I kissed her.

'Hey . . .'

'I love you . . .'

'And I love you.'

Love's the best fuck you can have. My heart was full of it, steaming like a cooking stew, running like the Master of the Cure. '. . . But I've got to go,' I said.

'Hurry back.'

'I will.'

'I'll be here.'

Estelle's father wouldn't let me in the hotel, so I kicked the door and shouted 'Fuck you!' at him, and said 'I wouldn't stay here,' at a couple of people who were humping their cases into the reception. 'You'll get food poisoning, and there's no heating in the bedrooms.' The couple looked at me, then looked at each other. 'Honestly,' I said, and then went back to the Beetle. I was about to get in when Clive ran down the steps towards me, calling, 'Duncan! Wait! Duncan!'

'Clive?'

'I've been waiting for you.'

'Where is she?'

'I don't know. She packed and left her cases in her room . . .'

'The cave.'

He scratched his head, buttoned his coat and said, 'I don't know.'

'Where else would she go?'

He shook his head. 'Come on,' he said.

We walked quickly, out of the car park, up the cliff path, past the bench and the grassy plateau to the first summit, and stopped to stand and survey the cliffs. They rose and fell like the backs of stranded animals, blinded by the sea. The swell was not as strong as it had been the day before, but when it slammed against the hidden coves below, the noise boomed up, shivering me. I looked at Clive and he looked at me; our eyes met and though we didn't say anything, words were exchanged. You can guess which ones, and you can sense the tone.

The air was fresh and cold, blowing onshore, whistling through the grass, sending high clouds flying across the sky. The sun was bright but not hot; the shadows of the clouds chased each other across the fields. We shaded our eyes and looked down the path. There was nobody out walking, there were no gulls flying over the cliffs, no mice scurrying through the bracken. You could believe that all the living things in the world had died, and the elements were gathering themselves, concentrating their powers while they considered their options. Was life worthwhile? Should we mix and match again? All that trouble and for what? All these questions, and none of them answered. They say life goes on, but it doesn't; only the elements go on. Clive walked on without talking. He took long steps, his eyes swivelling backwards and forwards, his nose pushed out like a dog's. Scents in the air or a movement in the grass no one would spot;

I followed him, I watched his back. It was like a blank map.

We didn't call for Mother, and as we walked, we went slower and slower, until by the time we had reached the abandoned mine, we were shuffling along. From a distance we would have looked as though we were barely moving, tiny solid figures painted against a perfect view. We came to the fenced shaft, ignored the warning signs and the crows that perched and cawed on the shattered walls, stepped over the broken wire and peered down.

The day did not steal the shaft's horror, but it lightened its edges and threw shadows down its sides, shadows that dropped into the gloom, highlighting the ledges, crevices and mosses that covered its sides. We stared down, and I shouted a useless 'MUM!' The word echoed below me, banged on the bottom and careered back at me. I was the gun and the word was the bullet; I shouted again, wings smacked above me, and the shadow of a crow passed over the shaft's rim. Clive put his hand on my shoulder and said, 'I don't think there's any point, Duncan, even if she was down there.'

'What makes you think she isn't?'

He shrugged. 'I don't know. Just a feeling.'

'Another feeling?'

'Yes,' he said.

I stood up straight and took a deep breath. He didn't take his hand from my shoulder. I could feel it cold through my coat. 'OK,' I said, 'then it's the cave.'

'I think so.'

'Come on then.'

'Yes,' he said, but he didn't move immediately. He stood and continued to stare down the shaft, as if there was something there, a clue, a sign, or a memory. He had a look in his eyes that reminded me, a look my father had often had. My mother inspired this concern in men, and she gave them more to worry about than you could carry. This worry nagged but could become an addictive thing, something close to pleasure. You were more than needed by her. She sucked herself in and sucked you in too; I see that now. I see too much that I missed, though it would be obvious to anyone else, I suppose. I suppose, because the narration of events gives things a sense they never had at the time. A pattern emerges that was never there or, if it was, it was hidden. The best things hide, but so do the worst; only the mediocre puts itself on permanent display. Clive would have had something to say about that idea, and I would have agreed with him, if for no other reason than a quiet life. I agreed with him like I agreed with Dad. I was afraid to argue, afraid that I would be shown up as an idiot. I got on with Dad, but since him, I haven't got on with other men. I suppose someone would tell me that that wasn't surprising, anyone with an ounce of sense would have predicted it. Of all the men in the world, Clive should have been the one I hated the most; he found my mother before I did, he was taking her away, he was this and that. He was so clever, so kind and had healing hands. Mother would follow him to Canada, but she wouldn't come with me to Exeter. Distance doesn't guarantee change or promise a new life; only a change of heart or thought does the trick. 'Trick' is the wrong word, but at that time, and under those circumstances, it was the only word I could think of.

I walked on from the mine, leading the way to the stone marker, the tree and the place where the path split. The wind was rattling the branches of the tree, throwing a noise like bones in a can into the air, a noise that made me shiver and wince. It took hold of my spine and twisted it slowly one way, then the other, then it ran its twiggy fingers up and down, so I felt myself buckle inside. This was a nasty feeling, but there was something pleasant about it too; I had to stop for a moment and support myself against the trunk. Clive came behind me and touched my elbow. 'Are you alright?' he said.

I nodded, but didn't say anything. I squinted around, he squeezed me gently and then I began to hurry down the path.

Now a feeling of panic had overtaken the resignation I had felt, it sped over me like the clouds, laid shadows on my back and began to press down. A wild, crazed feeling, and the sense that I was surfing, and that the ground was propelling me forward, rising up behind me and cresting over my head. The earth could have spat at me and I would not have been surprised, and the shrubs and grass could have turned to water all around me. A heavy swell began to heave beneath me, and my feet were caught in muddy currents that threatened to pull me down. An invisible reef was creasing the world and churning up eddies that swirled around my ankles; half way down the path I broke into a trot, and then I was running and I couldn't stop, and Clive was running behind me, his coat undone now and flapping like a big wing. I burst through the brambles and bracken, the sea tumbled and fell below us, I reached the rocks and boulders at the bottom, leapt over them with careless jumps, splashed through the rock-pools and slipped on to the beach. I fell face down in the sand. Clive came behind me, pulled me up and said, 'Alright?'

'Yeah.' I brushed my coat, wiped my hands and looked across the beach.

A single line of footprints lead across the sand from where we stood, breaking the otherwise perfect surface. The colours there were: yellow, blue, grey and white. The cove was sheltered from the wind that blew across the cliffs, so it was unnaturally warm there. At sea, a coaster steamed slowly across the horizon, a pencil of smoke seeping from its funnel. Clive sniffed the air, turned to me and said, 'She's here.'

I pointed at the footprints.

He said, 'They only go one way.'

I put my foot in one, then in another, then the next. Mother took very small steps, but she knew exactly where she was going. Her path curved towards the foot of the cliffs, around some weeded rocks and then across a patch of sand that lay like a terrace in front of her cave. My mother was sitting there, propped against a rock, staring out to sea. I started to run towards her, calling 'Mum! Mum!' and had got to within a few yards of her when I stopped. I felt Clive's hand on my arm, and he squeezed gently. The sea exploded around the offshore stacks and burst on to the beach. It ran up the sand and flowed around our feet; I looked down, then up again, and all I felt was a burning, as if my whole body had been torched, and flames were shooting from my eyes. Clive said, 'Steady, Duncan,' but the words were stolen by the wind and ripped into a thousand pieces. He relaxed his grip, I took three steps forward, and then went down on my knees.

My Mum's eyes were blue and reflected the sea, the sun and the sky, and the peace she felt. Her mouth was slightly open, her head was tipped to one side, and a breeze caressed her white and perfect cheeks. Her hair rustled, her nose was pink, and her ears were little shells. Only her neck looked unnatural; it was bent at a strange angle for a neck, and looked too smooth. Her right hand was resting on her lap, her left was lying on the rock, and the blood from her drained wrist was spread around her like a blanket. I reached out and touched her, and for a moment I could do nothing more; then I stood up and threw my arms around her, and hugged her as tightly as I could. I held and held, and I kissed her eyes. I think Clive stood next to me, but he could have been on another planet, in another time, he could have been another person. I prayed and I wished, I offered her my own life, I offered her all the things I love, I offered her a million hearts. I babbled whispers in her dead ears, and washed her face with my tears, but it was no good, no good at all. I screamed and shouted, and then gulls screamed back at me, and their shit rained down like confetti. All the surf in the world, all the dry and perfect waves barrelling into the sun could not help. I picked her up and I carried her back, and would not let anyone help me. Her blood was warm and it stained me. If it's the last thing I remember, and if it's the last thing I do.

How sad can you be, how bad and empty can things be before suicide is the only solution? As someone thinks about opening their veins, do they think about the people they will hurt, or is it the most selfish thing you can do? It can never be a cry for help, it can only be a silent shout. Raise your own hand against yourself and you betray your hand; your mind denies all the good you have ever done, it tries to prove that death is stronger than life, but it cannot. Suicide is a word from hell and echoes in hell every time it is spoken; I can accept my father's death, but Mum's left me as close to madness as a sane man can be.

All the accusations you expect came to call: I could have saved her, I should not have let her out of my sight, I wasn't strong enough for her, I am a weak man, I am responsible, how could I have been so stupid, all I needed was one more hour with her. Then angry thoughts: take your own life and ruin mine! Wives lose their husbands every second of every hour, what made your loss different? Are people going to say, 'Poor Diana, poor thing, she was so sad, we should have known, we should have cared!' No, Mother, they will not.

They will have forgotten about you. Only I have to carry the guilt and grief, from here to my grave, but don't worry. I'm hanging on for as long as I can. Life might be a bastard, but that's no reason to deny it a wedding.

NINETEEN

Estelle is asleep. I am standing by the window, looking down at a moonlit sea.

I started university, but dropped out after a term. I couldn't concentrate, the studies had no point, no meaning or sense, so I took the money Mother had left, and we moved in with Mrs Kertész. I do the heavy work around the house, and Estelle does the laundry and cleaning. We live in the attic bedroom with a view of the town, the harbour and the beach. Mrs Kertész treats us as her children and we treat her as a mother.

The best families are the ones that choose themselves. Nature is too cruel, too anxious to consume what it creates. It sows bad seed and it sows good; the bad protects itself, the good is exposed and hunted. Estelle turned in her sleep. I got in beside her and threaded my arm around her. A splinter of moonlight caught her face; she opened her eyes and smiled at me. 'Go back to sleep,' I said.

'You want me to?' she said.

'No.'

'What then?'

'You know . . .'

'Yes?'

'These things you keep,' I whispered, 'you better throw them away, turn your back on your soulless days . . .'

'What?' she said.

'Nothing.'

I stared at the ceiling and listened to her breathing. 'I want no wrinkle on your brow, no how . . .'

'Now what are you on about?'

'. . . because the sorrow of the past is all done, and the real happiness is just begun.'

'Duncan?'

'It's a song my Dad used to sing . . .' I said.

'Oh.'

'And I mean it.'

She looked at me, said, 'And I mean this,' and then as the moon was covered by cloud, she kissed my lips, ran her fingers through my hair and folded my body in the dark.